Myths of the Middle Ages

S. Baring-Gould

Myths of the Middle Ages

Copyright © 2024 Indo-European Publishing

All rights reserved

ISBN: 979-8-88942-425-3

CONTENTS

THE WANDERING JEW

WHO, that has looked on Gustave Doré's marvellous illustrations to this wild legend, can forget the impression they made upon his imagination?

I do not refer to the first illustration as striking, where the Jewish shoemaker is refusing to suffer the cross-laden Savior to rest a moment on his door-step, and is receiving with scornful lip the judgment to wander restless till the Second Coming of that same Redeemer. But I refer rather to the second, which represents the Jew, after the lapse of ages, bowed beneath the burden of the curse, worn with unrelieved toil, wearied with ceaseless travelling, trudging onward at the last lights of evening, when a rayless night of unabating rain is creeping on, along a sloppy path between dripping bushes; and suddenly he comes over against a wayside crucifix, on which the white glare of departing daylight falls, to throw it into ghastly relief against the pitch-black rain-clouds. For a moment we see the working of the miserable shoemaker's mind. We feel that he is recalling the tragedy of the first Good Friday, and his head hangs heavier on his breast, as he recalls the part he had taken in that awful catastrophe.

Or, is that other illustration more remarkable, where the wanderer is amongst the Alps, at the brink of a hideous chasm; and seeing in the contorted pine-branches the ever-haunting scene of the Via Dolorosa, he is lured to cast himself into that black gulf in quest of rest,—when an angel flashes out of the gloom with the sword of flame turning every way, keeping him back from what would be to him a Paradise indeed, the repose of Death?

Or, that last scene, when the trumpet sounds and earth is shivering to its foundations, the fire is bubbling forth through the rents in its surface, and the dead are coming together flesh to flesh, and bone to bone, and muscle to muscle—then the weary man sits down and casts off his shoes! Strange sights are around him, he sees them not; strange sounds assail his ears, he hears but one—the trumpet-note which gives the signal for him to stay his wanderings and rest his weary feet.

I can linger over those noble woodcuts, and learn from them something new each time that I study them; they are picture-poems full of latent depths of thought. And now let us to the history of this most thrilling of all mediæval myths, if a myth.

If a myth, I say, for who can say for certain that it is not true? "Verily I say unto you, There be some standing here, which shall not taste of death till they see the Son of Man coming in His kingdom,"[1] are our Lord's words, which I can hardly think apply to the destruction of Jerusalem, as commentators explain it to escape the difficulty. That some should live to see Jerusalem destroyed was not very surprising, and hardly needed the emphatic Verily which Christ only used when speaking something of peculiarly solemn or mysterious import.

Besides, St. Luke's account manifestly refers the coming in the kingdom to the Judgment, for the saying stands as follows: "Whosoever shall be ashamed of Me, and of My words, of him shall the Son of Man be ashamed, when He shall come in His own glory, and in His Father's, and of the holy angels. But I tell you of a truth, there be some standing here, which shall not taste of death till they see the kingdom of God."[2]

There can, I think, be no doubt in the mind of an unprejudiced person that the words of our Lord do imply that some one or more of those then living should not die till He came again. I do not mean to insist on the literal signification, but I plead that there is no improbability in our Lord's words being fulfilled to the letter. That the circumstance is unrecorded in the Gospels is no evidence that it did not take place, for we are expressly told, "Many other signs truly did Jesus in the presence of His disciples, which are not written in this book;"[3] and again, "There are also many other things which Jesus did, the which, if they should be written every one, I

---

[1] Matt. xvi. 28. Mark ix. 1.

[2] Luke ix.

[3] John xx. 30.

suppose that even the world itself could not contain the books that should be written."[4]

We may remember also the mysterious witnesses who are to appear in the last eventful days of the world's history and bear testimony to the Gospel truth before the antichristian world. One of these has been often conjectured to be St. John the Evangelist, of whom Christ said to Peter, "If I will that he tarry till I come, what is that to thee?"

The historical evidence on which the tale rests is, however, too slender for us to admit for it more than the barest claim to be more than myth. The names and the circumstances connected with the Jew and his doom vary in every account, and the only point upon which all coincide is, that such an individual exists in an undying condition, wandering over the face of the earth, seeking rest and finding none.

The earliest extant mention of the Wandering Jew is to be found in the book of the chronicles of the Abbey of St. Albans, which was copied and continued by Matthew Paris. He records that in the year 1228, "a certain Archbishop of Armenia the Greater came on a pilgrimage to England to see the relics of the saints, and visit the sacred places in the kingdom, as he had done in others; he also produced letters of recommendation from his Holiness the Pope, to the religious and the prelates of the churches, in which they were enjoined to receive and entertain him with due reverence and honor. On his arrival, he came to St. Albans, where he was received with all respect by the abbot and the monks; and at this place, being fatigued with his journey, he remained some days to rest himself and his followers, and a conversation took place between him and the inhabitants of the convent, by means of their interpreters, during which he made many inquiries relating to the religion and religious observances of this country, and told many strange things concerning the countries of the East. In the course of conversation he was asked whether he had ever seen or heard any thing of Joseph, a man of whom there was much talk in the world, who, when our Lord suffered, was present and spoke to Him, and

____

4 John xxi. 25.

who is still alive, in evidence of the Christian faith; in reply to which, a knight in his retinue, who was his interpreter, replied, speaking in French, 'My lord well knows that man, and a little before he took his way to the western countries, the said Joseph ate at the table of my lord the Archbishop of Armenia, and he has often seen and conversed with him.'

"He was then asked about what had passed between Christ and the said Joseph; to which he replied, 'At the time of the passion of Jesus Christ, He was seized by the Jews, and led into the hall of judgment before Pilate, the governor, that He might be judged by him on the accusation of the Jews; and Pilate, finding no fault for which he might sentence Him to death, said unto them, "Take Him and judge Him according to your law;" the shouts of the Jews, however, increasing, he, at their request, released unto them Barabbas, and delivered Jesus to them to be crucified. When, therefore, the Jews were dragging Jesus forth, and had reached the door, Cartaphilus, a porter of the hall in Pilate's service, as Jesus was going out of the door, impiously struck Him on the back with his hand, and said in mockery, "Go quicker, Jesus, go quicker; why do you loiter?" and Jesus, looking back on him with a severe countenance, said to him, "I am going, and you shall wait till I return." And according as our Lord said, this Cartaphilus is still awaiting His return. At the time of our Lord's suffering he was thirty years old, and when he attains the age of a hundred years, he always returns to the same age as he was when our Lord suffered. After Christ's death, when the Catholic faith gained ground, this Cartaphilus was baptized by Ananias (who also baptized the Apostle Paul), and was called Joseph. He dwells in one or other divisions of Armenia, and in divers Eastern countries, passing his time amongst the bishops and other prelates of the Church; he is a man of holy conversation, and religious; a man of few words, and very circumspect in his behavior; for he does not speak at all unless when questioned by the bishops and religious; and then he relates the events of olden times, and speaks of things which occurred at the suffering and resurrection of our Lord, and of the witnesses of the resurrection, namely, of those who rose with Christ, and went into the holy city, and appeared unto men. He also tells of the creed of the Apostles, and of their separation and preaching. And all this he relates without smiling, or levity of conversation, as one who is well practised in sorrow and the fear of God, always looking forward with dread to the coming of Jesus Christ, lest at the Last Judgment he should find him in anger whom, when on his way to death, he had provoked to just vengeance. Numbers came to him from different parts of the world, enjoying his society and conversation; and to them, if they are men of authority, he explains all doubts on the matters on which he is questioned. He refuses all gifts that are offered him, being content with slight food and clothing.'"

Much about the same date, Philip Mouskes, afterwards Bishop of Tournay, wrote his rhymed chronicle (1242), which contains a similar account of the Jew, derived from the same Armenian prelate:—

> "Adonques vint un arceveskes
> De çà mer, plains de bonnes tèques
> Par samblant, et fut d'Armenie,"

and this man, having visited the shrine of "St. Tumas de Kantorbire," and then having paid his devotions at "Monsigour St. Jake," he went on to Cologne to see the heads of the three kings. The version told in the Netherlands much resembled that related at St. Albans, only that the Jew, seeing the people dragging Christ to his death, exclaims,—

> "Atendés moi! g'i vois,
> S'iert mis le faus profète en crois."

Then

> "Le vrais Dieux se regarda,
> Et li a dit qu'e n'i tarda,
> Icist ne t'atenderont pas,
> Mais saces, tu m'atenderas."

We hear no more of the wandering Jew till the sixteenth century, when we hear first of him in a casual manner, as assisting a weaver, Kokot, at the royal palace in Bohemia (1505), to find a treasure which had been secreted by the great-grandfather of Kokot, sixty years before, at which time the Jew was present. He then had the appearance of being a man of seventy years.[5]

Curiously enough, we next hear of him in the East, where he is confounded with the prophet Elijah. Early in the century he appeared to Fadhilah, under peculiar circumstances.

After the Arabs had captured the city of Elvan, Fadhilah, at the head of three hundred horsemen, pitched his tents, late in the evening, between two mountains. Fadhilah, having begun his evening prayer with a loud voice, heard the words "Allah akbar" (God is great) repeated distinctly, and each word of his prayer was followed in a similar manner. Fadhilah, not believing this to be the result of an echo, was much astonished, and cried out, "O thou! whether thou art of the angel ranks, or whether thou art of some other order of spirits, it is well; the power of God be with thee; but if thou art a man, then let mine eyes light upon thee, that I may rejoice in thy presence and society." Scarcely had he spoken these words, before an aged man, with bald head, stood before him, holding a staff in his hand, and much resembling a dervish in appearance. After having courteously saluted him, Fadhilah asked the old man who he was. Thereupon the stranger answered, "Bassi Hadhret Issa, I am here by command of the Lord Jesus, who has left me in this world, that I may live therein until he comes a second time to earth. I wait for this Lord, who is the Fountain of Happiness, and in obedience to his command I dwell behind yon mountain." When Fadhilah heard these words, he asked when the Lord Jesus would appear; and the old man replied that his appearing would be at the end of the world, at the Last Judgment. But this only increased Fadhilah's curiosity, so that he inquired the signs of the approach of the end of all things, whereupon Zerib Bar

---

[5] Gubitz, Gesellsch. 1845, No. 18.

Elia gave him an account of general, social, and moral dissolution, which would be the climax of this world's history.[6]

In 1547 he was seen in Europe, if we are to believe the following narration:—

"Paul von Eitzen, doctor of the Holy Scriptures, and Bishop of Schleswig,[7] related as true for some years past, that when he was young, having studied at Wittemberg, he returned home to his parents in Hamburg in the winter of the year 1547, and that on the following Sunday, in church, he observed a tall man, with his hair hanging over his shoulders, standing barefoot, during the sermon, over against the pulpit, listening with deepest attention to the discourse, and, whenever the name of Jesus was mentioned, bowing himself profoundly and humbly, with sighs and beating of the breast. He had no other clothing, in the bitter cold of the winter, except a pair of hose which were in tatters about his feet, and a coat with a girdle which reached to his feet; and his general appearance was that of a man of fifty years. And many people, some of high degree and title, have seen this same man in England, France, Italy, Hungary, Persia, Spain, Poland, Moscow, Lapland, Sweden, Denmark, Scotland, and other places.

"Every one wondered over the man. Now, after the sermon, the said Doctor inquired diligently where the stranger was to be found; and when he had sought him out, he inquired of him privately whence he came, and how long that winter he had been in the place. Thereupon he replied, modestly, that he was a Jew by birth, a native of Jerusalem, by name Ahasverus, by trade a shoemaker; he had been present at the crucifixion of Christ, and had lived ever since, travelling through various lands and cities, the which he substantiated by accounts he gave; he related also the circumstances of Christ's transference from Pilate to Herod, and the final crucifixion, together with other details not recorded in the Evangelists and historians; he gave accounts of the changes of

---

[6] Herbelot, Bibl. Orient, iii. p. 607.

[7] Paul v. Eitzen was born January 25, 1522, at Hamburg; in 1562 he was appointed chief preacher for Schleswig, and died February 25, 1598. (Greve, Memor. P. ab. Eitzen. Hamb. 1844.)

government in many countries, especially of the East, through several centuries; and moreover he detailed the labors and deaths of the holy Apostles of Christ most circumstantially.

"Now when Doctor Paul v. Eitzen heard this with profound astonishment, on account of its incredible novelty, he inquired further, in order that he might obtain more accurate information. Then the man answered, that he had lived in Jerusalem at the time of the crucifixion of Christ, whom he had regarded as a deceiver of the people, and a heretic; he had seen Him with his own eyes, and had done his best, along with others, to bring this deceiver, as he regarded Him, to justice, and to have Him put out of the way. When the sentence had been pronounced by Pilate, Christ was about to be dragged past his house; then he ran home, and called together his household to have a look at Christ, and see what sort of a person He was.

"This having been done, he had his little child on his arm, and was standing in his doorway, to have a sight of the Lord Jesus Christ.

"As, then, Christ was led by, bowed under the weight of the heavy cross, He tried to rest a little, and stood still a moment; but the shoemaker, in zeal and rage, and for the sake of obtaining credit among the other Jews, drove the Lord Christ forward, and told Him to hasten on His way. Jesus, obeying, looked at him, and said, 'I shall stand and rest, but thou shalt go till the last day.' At these words the man set down the child; and, unable to remain where he was, he followed Christ, and saw how cruelly He was crucified, how He suffered, how He died. As soon as this had taken place, it came upon him suddenly that he could no more return to Jerusalem, nor see again his wife and child, but must go forth into foreign lands, one after another, like a mournful pilgrim. Now, when, years after, he returned to Jerusalem, he found it ruined and utterly razed, so that not one stone was left standing on another; and he could not recognize former localities.

"He believes that it is God's purpose, in thus driving him about in miserable life, and preserving him undying, to present him before the Jews at the end, as a living token, so that the godless and unbelieving may remember the death of Christ, and be turned to repentance. For his part he would well rejoice were God in heaven to release him from this vale of tears. After this conversation, Doctor Paul v. Eitzen, along with the rector of the school of Hamburg, who was well read in history, and a traveller, questioned him about events which had taken place in the East since the death of Christ, and he was able to give them much information on many ancient matters; so that it was impossible not to be convinced of the truth of his story, and to see that what seems impossible with men is, after all, possible with God.

"Since the Jew has had his life extended, he has become silent and reserved, and only answers direct questions. When invited to become any one's guest, he eats little, and drinks in great moderation; then hurries on, never remaining long in one place. When at Hamburg, Dantzig, and elsewhere, money has been offered him, he never took more than two skillings (fourpence, one farthing), and at once distributed it to the poor, as token that he needed no money, for God would provide for him, as he rued the sins he had committed in ignorance.

"During the period of his stay in Hamburg and Dantzig he was never seen to laugh. In whatever land he travelled he spoke its language, and when he spoke Saxon, it was like a native Saxon. Many people came from different places to Hamburg and Dantzig in order to see and hear this man, and were convinced that the providence of God was exercised in this individual in a very remarkable manner. He gladly listened to God's word, or heard it spoken of always with great gravity and compunction, and he ever reverenced with sighs the pronunciation of the name of God, or of Jesus Christ, and could not endure to hear curses; but whenever he heard any one swear by God's death or pains, he waxed indignant, and exclaimed, with vehemence and with sighs, 'Wretched man and miserable creature, thus to misuse the name of thy Lord and God, and His bitter sufferings and passion. Hadst thou seen, as I have, how heavy and bitter were the pangs and wounds of thy Lord, endured for thee and for me, thou wouldst rather undergo great pain thyself than thus take His sacred name in vain!'

"Such is the account given to me by Doctor Paul von Eitzen, with many circumstantial proofs, and corroborated by certain of my own old acquaintances who saw this same individual with their own eyes in Hamburg.

"In the year 1575 the Secretary Christopher Krause, and Master Jacob von Holstein, legates to the Court of Spain, and afterwards sent into the Netherlands to pay the soldiers serving his Majesty in that country, related on their return home to Schleswig, and confirmed with solemn oaths, that they had come across the same mysterious individual at Madrid in Spain, in appearance, manner of life, habits, clothing, just the same as he had appeared in Hamburg. They said that they had spoken with him, and that many people of all classes had conversed with him, and found him to speak good Spanish. In the year 1599, in December, a reliable person wrote from Brunswick to Strasburg that the same mentioned strange person had been seen alive at Vienna in Austria, and that he had started for Poland and Dantzig; and that he purposed going on to Moscow. This Ahasverus was at Lubeck in 1601, also about the same date in Revel in Livonia, and in Cracow in Poland. In Moscow he was seen of many and spoken to by many.

"What thoughtful, God-fearing persons are to think of the said person, is at their option. God's works are wondrous and past finding out, and are manifested day by day, only to be revealed in full at the last great day of account.

"Dated, Revel, August 1st, 1613.
"D. W.
"D.
"Chrysostomus Duduloeus,
"Westphalus."

The statement that the Wandering Jew appeared in Lubeck in 1601, does not tally with the more precise chronicle of Henricus Bangert, which gives: "Die 14 Januarii Anno MDCIII., adnotatum reliquit Lubecæ fuisse Judæum illum immortalem, qui se Christi crucifixioni interfuisse affirmavit."[8]

In 1604 he seems to have appeared in Paris. Rudolph Botoreus says, under this date, "I fear lest I be accused of giving ear to old

---

[8] Henr. Bangert, Comment. De Ortu, Vita, et Excessu Coleri, I. Cti. Lubec.

wives' fables, if I insert in these pages what is reported all over Europe of the Jew, coeval with the Savior Christ; however, nothing is more common, and our popular histories have not scrupled to assert it. Following the lead of those who wrote our annals, I may say that he who appeared not in one century only, in Spain, Italy, and Germany, was also in this year seen and recognized as the same individual who had appeared in Hamburg, anno MDLXVI. The common people, bold in spreading reports, relate many things of him; and this I allude to, lest anything should be left unsaid."[9]

J. C. Bulenger puts the date of the Hamburg visit earlier. "It was reported at this time that a Jew of the time of Christ was wandering without food and drink, having for a thousand and odd years been a vagabond and outcast, condemned by God to rove, because he, of that generation of vipers, was the first to cry out for the crucifixion of Christ and the release of Barabbas; and also because soon after, when Christ, panting under the burden of the rood, sought to rest before his workshop (he was a cobbler), the fellow ordered Him off with acerbity. Thereupon Christ replied, 'Because thou grudgest Me such a moment of rest, I shall enter into My rest, but thou shalt wander restless.' At once, frantic and agitated, he fled through the whole earth, and on the same account to this day he journeys through the world. It was this person who was seen in Hamburg in MDLXIV. Credat Judæus Apella! I did not see him, or hear anything authentic concerning him, at that time when I was in Paris."[10]

A curious little book,[11] written against the quackery of Paracelsus, by Leonard Doldius, a Nürnberg physician, and translated into Latin and augmented, by Andreas Libavius, doctor and physician of Rotenburg, alludes to the same story, and gives the Jew a new name nowhere else met with. After having referred to a report that Paracelsus was not dead, but was seated alive, asleep or napping, in his sepulchre at Strasburg, preserved from death by some of his specifics, Libavius declares that he would

---

[9] R. Botoreus, Comm. Histor. lii. p. 305.

[10] J. C. Bulenger, Historia sui Temporis, p. 357.

[11] Praxis Alchymiæ. Francfurti, MDCIV. 8vo.

sooner believe in the old man, the Jew, Ahasverus, wandering over the world, called by some Buttadæus, and otherwise, again, by others.

He is said to have appeared in Naumburg, but the date is not given; he was noticed in church, listening to the sermon. After the service he was questioned, and he related his story. On this occasion he received presents from the burgers.[12] In 1633 he was again in Hamburg.[13] In the year 1640, two citizens, living in the Gerberstrasse, in Brussels, were walking in the Sonian wood, when they encountered an aged man, whose clothes were in tatters and of an antiquated appearance. They invited him to go with them to a house of refreshment, and he went with them, but would not seat himself, remaining on foot to drink. When he came before the doors with the two burgers, he told them a great deal; but they were mostly stories of events which had happened many hundred years before. Hence the burgers gathered that their companion was Isaac Laquedem, the Jew who had refused to permit our Blessed Lord to rest for a moment at his door-step, and they left him full of terror. In 1642 he is reported to have visited Leipzig. On the 22d July, 1721, he appeared at the gates of the city of Munich.[14] About the end of the seventeenth century or the beginning of the eighteenth, an impostor, calling himself the Wandering Jew, attracted attention in England, and was listened to by the ignorant, and despised by the educated. He, however, managed to thrust himself into the notice of the nobility, who, half in jest, half in curiosity, questioned him, and paid him as they might a juggler. He declared that he had been an officer of the Sanhedrim, and that he had struck Christ as he left the judgment hall of Pilate. He remembered all the Apostles, and described their personal appearance, their clothes, and their peculiarities. He spoke many languages, claimed the power of healing the sick, and asserted that he had travelled nearly all over the world. Those who heard him were perplexed by his familiarity with foreign tongues and places. Oxford and Cambridge sent

---

[12] Mitternacht, Diss. in Johann. xxi. 19.

[13] Mitternacht, ut supra.

[14] Hormayr, Taschenbuch, 1834, p. 216.

professors to question him, and to discover the imposition, if any. An English nobleman conversed with him in Arabic. The mysterious stranger told his questioner in that language that historical works were not to be relied upon. And on being asked his opinion of Mahomet, he replied that he had been acquainted with the father of the prophet, and that he dwelt at Ormuz. As for Mahomet, he believed him to have been a man of intelligence; once when he heard the prophet deny that Christ was crucified, he answered abruptly by telling him he was a witness to the truth of that event. He related also that he was in Rome when Nero set it on fire; he had known Saladin, Tamerlane, Bajazeth, Eterlane, and could give minute details of the history of the Crusades.[15]

Whether this wandering Jew was found out in London or not, we cannot tell, but he shortly after appeared in Denmark, thence travelled into Sweden, and vanished.

Such are the principal notices of the Wandering Jew which have appeared. It will be seen at once how wanting they are in all substantial evidence which could make us regard the story in any other light than myth.

But no myth is wholly without foundation, and there must be some substantial verity upon which this vast superstructure of legend has been raised. What that is I am unable to discover.

It has been suggested by some that the Jew Ahasverus is an impersonation of that race which wanders, Cain-like, over the earth with the brand of a brother's blood upon it, and one which is not to pass away till all be fulfilled, not to be reconciled to its angered God till the times of the Gentiles are accomplished. And yet, probable as this supposition may seem at first sight, it is not to be harmonized with some of the leading features of the story. The shoemaker becomes a penitent, and earnest Christian, whilst the Jewish nation has still the veil upon its heart; the wretched wanderer eschews money, and the avarice of the Israelite is proverbial.

According to local legend, he is identified with the Gypsies, or rather that strange people are supposed to be living under a curse somewhat similar to that inflicted on Ahasverus, because they

---

[15] Calmet, Dictionn. de la Bible, t. ii. p. 472

refused shelter to the Virgin and Child on their flight into Egypt.[16] Another tradition connects the Jew with the wild huntsman, and there is a forest at Bretten, in Swabia, which he is said to haunt. Popular superstition attributes to him there a purse containing a groschen, which, as often as it is expended, returns to the spender.[17]

In the Harz one form of the Wild Huntsman myth is to this effect: that he was a Jew who had refused to suffer our Blessed Lord to drink out of a river, or out of a horse-trough, but had contemptuously pointed out to Him the hoof-print of a horse, in which a little water had collected, and had bid Him quench His thirst thence.[18]

As the Wild Huntsman is the personification of the storm, it is curious to find in parts of France that the sudden roar of a gale at night is attributed by the vulgar to the passing of the Everlasting Jew.

A Swiss story is, that he was seen one day standing upon the Matterberg, which is below the Matterhorn, contemplating the scene with mingled sorrow and wonder. Once before he stood on that spot, and then it was the site of a flourishing city; now it is covered with gentian and wild pinks. Once again will he revisit the hill, and that will be on the eve of Judgment.

Perhaps, of all the myths which originated in the middle ages, none is more striking than that we have been considering; indeed, there is something so calculated to arrest the attention and to excite the imagination in the outline of the story, that it is remarkable that we should find an interval of three centuries elapse between its first introduction into Europe by Matthew Paris and Philip Mouskes, and its general acceptance in the sixteenth century. As a myth, its roots lie in that great mystery of human life which is an enigma never solved, and ever originating speculation.

What was life? Was it of necessity limited to fourscore years, or could it be extended indefinitely? Were questions curious minds never wearied of asking. And so the mythology of the past teemed

---

¹⁶ Aventinus, Bayr. Chronik, viii.

¹⁷ Meier, Schwäbischen Sagen, i. 116

¹⁸ Kuhn u. Schwarz Nordd. Sagen, p. 499

with legends of favored or accursed mortals, who had reached beyond the term of days set to most men. Some had discovered the water of life, the fountain of perpetual youth, and were ever renewing their strength. Others had dared the power of God, and were therefore sentenced to feel the weight of His displeasure, without tasting the repose of death.

John the Divine slept at Ephesus, untouched by corruption, with the ground heaving over his breast as he breathed, waiting the summons to come forth and witness against Antichrist. The seven sleepers reposed in a cave, and centuries glided by like a watch in the night. The monk of Hildesheim, doubting how with God a thousand years could be as yesterday, listened to the melody of a bird in the green wood during three minutes, and found that in three minutes three hundred years had flown. Joseph of Arimathæa, in the blessed city of Sarras, draws perpetual life from the Saint Graal; Merlin sleeps and sighs in an old tree, spell-bound of Vivien. Charlemagne and Barbarossa wait, crowned and armed, in the heart of the mountain, till the time comes for the release of Fatherland from despotism. And, on the other hand, the curse of a deathless life has passed on the Wild Huntsman, because he desired to chase the red-deer for evermore; on the Captain of the Phantom Ship, because he vowed he would double the Cape whether God willed it or not; on the Man in the Moon, because he gathered sticks during the Sabbath rest; on the dancers of Kolbeck, because they desired to spend eternity in their mad gambols.

I began this article intending to conclude it with a bibliographical account of the tracts, letters, essays, and books, written upon the Wandering Jew; but I relinquish my intention at the sight of the multitude of works which have issued from the press upon the subject; and this I do with less compunction as the bibliographer may at little trouble and expense satisfy himself, by perusing the lists given by Grässe in his essay on the myth, and those to be found in "Notice historique et bibliographique sur les Juifs-errants: par O. B." (Gustave Brunet), Paris, Téchener, 1845; also in the article by M. Mangin, in "Causeries et Méditations historiques et littéraires," Paris, Duprat, 1843; and, lastly, in the essay by Jacob le Bibliophile (M. Lacroix) in his "Curiosités de l'Histoire des Croyances populaires," Paris, Delahays, 1859.

Of the romances of Eugène Sue and Dr. Croly, founded upon the legend, the less said the better. The original legend is so noble in its severe simplicity, that none but a master mind could develop it with any chance of success. Nor have the poetical attempts upon the story fared better. It was reserved for the pencil of Gustave Doré to treat it with the originality it merited, and in a series of woodcuts to produce at once a poem, a romance, and a chef-d'œuvre of art.

PRESTER JOHN

ABOUT the middle of the twelfth century, a rumor circulated through Europe that there reigned in Asia a powerful Christian Emperor, Presbyter Johannes. In a bloody fight he had broken the power of the Mussulmans, and was ready to come to the assistance of the Crusaders. Great was the exultation in Europe, for of late the news from the East had been gloomy and depressing, the power of the infidel had increased, overwhelming masses of men had been brought into the field against the chivalry of Christendom, and it was felt that the cross must yield before the odious crescent.

The news of the success of the Priest-King opened a door of hope to the desponding Christian world. Pope Alexander III. determined at once to effect a union with this mysterious personage, and on the 27th of September, 1177, wrote him a letter, which he intrusted to his physician, Philip, to deliver in person.

Philip started on his embassy, but never returned. The conquests of Tschengis-Khan again attracted the eyes of Christian Europe to the East. The Mongol hordes were rushing in upon the west with devastating ferocity; Russia, Poland, Hungary, and the eastern provinces of Germany, had succumbed, or suffered grievously; and the fears of other nations were roused lest they too should taste the misery of a Mongolian invasion. It was Gog and Magog come to slaughter, and the times of Antichrist were dawning. But the battle of Liegnitz stayed them in their onward career, and Europe was saved.

Pope Innocent IV. determined to convert these wild hordes of barbarians, and subject them to the cross of Christ; he therefore sent among them a number of Dominican and Franciscan missioners, and embassies of peace passed between the Pope, the King of France, and the Mogul Khan.

The result of these communications with the East was, that the travellers learned how false were the prevalent notions of a mighty Christian empire existing in Central Asia. Vulgar superstition or conviction is not, however, to be upset by evidence, and the locality of the monarchy was merely transferred by the people to Africa, and they fixed upon Abyssinia, with a show of truth, as the seat of the famous Priest-King. However, still some doubted. John de Plano Carpini and Marco Polo, though they acknowledged the existence of a Christian monarch in Abyssinia, yet stoutly maintained as well that the Prester John of popular belief reigned in splendor somewhere in the dim Orient.

But before proceeding with the history of this strange fable, it will be well to extract the different accounts given of the Priest-King and his realm by early writers; and we shall then be better able to judge of the influence the myth obtained in Europe.

Otto of Freisingen is the first author to mention the monarchy of Prester John with whom we are acquainted. Otto wrote a chronicle up to the date 1156, and he relates that in 1145 the Catholic Bishop of Cabala visited Europe to lay certain complaints before the Pope. He mentioned the fall of Edessa, and also "he stated that a few years ago a certain King and Priest called John, who lives on the farther side of Persia and Armenia, in the remote East, and who, with all his people, were Christians, though belonging to the Nestorian Church, had overcome the royal brothers Samiardi, kings of the Medes and Persians, and had captured Ecbatana, their capital and residence. The said kings had met with their Persian, Median, and Assyrian troops, and had fought for three consecutive days, each side having determined to die rather than take to flight. Prester John, for so they are wont to call him, at length routed the Persians, and after a bloody battle, remained victorious. After which victory the said John was hastening to the assistance of the Church at Jerusalem, but his host, on reaching the Tigris, was hindered from passing, through a deficiency in boats, and he directed his march North, since he had heard that the river was there covered with ice. In that place he had waited many years, expecting severe cold; but the winters having proved unpropitious, and the severity of the climate having carried off many soldiers, he had been forced to retreat to his own land. This king belongs to the family of the Magi, mentioned in the Gospel, and he rules over the very people formerly governed by the

Magi; moreover, his fame and his wealth are so great, that he uses an emerald sceptre only.

"Excited by the example of his ancestors, who came to worship Christ in his cradle, he had proposed to go to Jerusalem, but had been impeded by the above-mentioned causes."[19]

At the same time the story crops up in other quarters; so that we cannot look upon Otto as the inventor of the myth. The celebrated Maimonides alludes to it in a passage quoted by Joshua Lorki, a Jewish physician to Benedict XIII. Maimonides lived from 1135 to 1204. The passage is as follows: "It is evident both from the letters of Rambam (Maimonides), whose memory be blessed, and from the narration of merchants who have visited the ends of the earth, that at this time the root of our faith is to be found in the lands of Babel and Teman, where long ago Jerusalem was an exile; not reckoning those who live in the land of Paras[20] and Madai,[21] of the exiles of Schomrom, the number of which people is as the sand: of these some are still under the yoke of Paras, who is called the Great-Chief Sultan by the Arabs; others live in a place under the yoke of a strange people ... governed by a Christian chief, Preste-Cuan by name. With him they have made a compact, and he with them; and this is a matter concerning which there can be no manner of doubt."

Benjamin of Tudela, another Jew, travelled in the East between the years 1159 and 1173, the last being the date of his death. He wrote an account of his travels, and gives in it some information with regard to a mythical Jew king, who reigned in the utmost splendor over a realm inhabited by Jews alone, situate somewhere in the midst of a desert of vast extent. About this period there appeared a document which produced intense excitement throughout Europe—a letter, yes! a letter from the mysterious personage himself to Manuel Comnenus, Emperor of Constantinople (1143-1180). The exact date of this extraordinary epistle cannot be fixed with any certainty, but it certainly appeared

---

[19] Otto, Ep. Frising., lib. vii. c. 33.
[20] Persia.
[21] Media.

before 1241, the date of the conclusion of the chronicle of Albericus Trium Fontium. This Albericus relates that in the year 1165 "Presbyter Joannes, the Indian king, sent his wonderful letter to various Christian princes, and especially to Manuel of Constantinople, and Frederic the Roman Emperor." Similar letters were sent to Alexander III., to Louis VII. of France, and to the King of Portugal, which are alluded to in chronicles and romances, and which were indeed turned into rhyme, and sung all over Europe by minstrels and trouvères. The letter is as follows:—

"John, Priest by the Almighty power of God and the Might of our Lord Jesus Christ, King of Kings, and Lord of Lords, to his friend Emanuel, Prince of Constantinople, greeting, wishing him health, prosperity, and the continuance of Divine favor.

"Our Majesty has been informed that you hold our Excellency in love, and that the report of our greatness has reached you. Moreover, we have heard through our treasurer that you have been pleased to send to us some objects of art and interest, that our Exaltedness might be gratified thereby.

"Being human, I receive it in good part, and we have ordered our treasurer to send you some of our articles in return.

"Now we desire to be made certain that you hold the right faith, and in all things cleave to Jesus Christ, our Lord, for we have heard that your court regard you as a god, though we know that you are mortal, and subject to human infirmities.... Should you desire to learn the greatness and excellency of our Exaltedness and of the land subject to our sceptre, then hear and believe:—I, Presbyter Johannes, the Lord of Lords, surpass all under heaven in virtue, in riches, and in power; seventy-two kings pay us tribute.... In the three Indies our Magnificence rules, and our land extends beyond India, where rests the body of the holy Apostle Thomas; it reaches towards the sunrise over the wastes, and it trends towards deserted Babylon near the tower of Babel. Seventy-two provinces, of which only a few are Christian, serve us. Each has its own king, but all are tributary to us.

"Our land is the home of elephants, dromedaries, camels, crocodiles, meta-collinarum, cametennus, tensevetes, wild asses, white and red lions, white bears, white merules, crickets, griffins,

tigers, lamias, hyenas, wild horses, wild oxen and wild men, men
with horns, one-eyed, men with eyes before and behind, centaurs,
fauns, satyrs, pygmies, forty-ell-high giants, Cyclopses, and similar
women; it is the home, too, of the phœnix, and of nearly all living
animals. We have some people subject to us who feed on the flesh
of men and of prematurely born animals, and who never fear death.
When any of these people die, their friends and relations eat him
ravenously, for they regard it as a main duty to munch human
flesh. Their names are Gog and Magog, Anie, Agit, Azenach,
Fommeperi, Befari, Conei-Samante, Agrimandri, Vintefolei, Casbei,
Alanei. These and similar nations were shut in behind lofty
mountains by Alexander the Great, towards the North. We lead
them at our pleasure against our foes, and neither man nor beast is
left undevoured, if our Majesty gives the requisite permission. And
when all our foes are eaten, then we return with our hosts home
again. These accursed fifteen nations will burst forth from the four
quarters of the earth at the end of the world, in the times of
Antichrist, and overrun all the abodes of the Saints as well as the
great city Rome, which, by the way, we are prepared to give to our
son who will be born, along with all Italy, Germany, the two Gauls,
Britain and Scotland. We shall also give him Spain and all the land
as far as the icy sea. The nations to which I have alluded, according
to the words of the prophet, shall not stand in the judgment, on
account of their offensive practices, but will be consumed to ashes
by a fire which will fall on them from heaven.

"Our land streams with honey, and is overflowing with milk.
In one region grows no poisonous herb, nor does a querulous frog
ever quack in it; no scorpion exists, nor does the serpent glide
amongst the grass, nor can any poisonous animals exist in it, or
injure any one.

"Among the heathen, flows through a certain province the
River Indus; encircling Paradise, it spreads its arms in manifold
windings through the entire province. Here are found the emeralds,
sapphires, carbuncles, topazes, chrysolites, onyxes, beryls, sardius,
and other costly stones. Here grows the plant Assidos, which, when
worn by any one, protects him from the evil spirit, forcing it to state
its business and name; consequently the foul spirits keep out of the

way there. In a certain land subject to us, all kinds of pepper is gathered, and is exchanged for corn and bread, leather and cloth.... At the foot of Mount Olympus bubbles up a spring which changes its flavor hour by hour, night and day, and the spring is scarcely three days' journey from Paradise, out of which Adam was driven. If any one has tasted thrice of the fountain, from that day he will feel no fatigue, but will, as long as he lives, be as a man of thirty years. Here are found the small stones called Nudiosi, which, if borne about the body, prevent the sight from waxing feeble, and restore it where it is lost. The more the stone is looked at, the keener becomes the sight. In our territory is a certain waterless sea, consisting of tumbling billows of sand never at rest. None have crossed this sea; it lacks water altogether, yet fish are cast up upon the beach of various kinds, very tasty, and the like are nowhere else to be seen. Three days' journey from this sea are mountains from which rolls down a stony, waterless river, which opens into the sandy sea. As soon as the stream reaches the sea, its stones vanish in it, and are never seen again. As long as the river is in motion, it cannot be crossed; only four days a week is it possible to traverse it. Between the sandy sea and the said mountains, in a certain plain is a fountain of singular virtue, which purges Christians and would-be Christians from all transgressions. The water stands four inches high in a hollow stone shaped like a mussel-shell. Two saintly old men watch by it, and ask the comers whether they are Christians, or are about to become Christians, then whether they desire healing with all their hearts. If they have answered well, they are bidden to lay aside their clothes, and to step into the mussel. If what they said be true, then the water begins to rise and gush over their heads; thrice does the water thus lift itself, and every one who has entered the mussel leaves it cured of every complaint.

"Near the wilderness trickles between barren mountains a subterranean rill, which can only by chance be reached, for only occasionally the earth gapes, and he who would descend must do it with precipitation, ere the earth closes again. All that is gathered under the ground there is gem and precious stone. The brook pours into another river, and the inhabitants of the neighborhood obtain thence abundance of precious stones. Yet they never venture to sell them without having first offered them to us for our private use: should we decline them, they are at liberty to dispose of them to strangers. Boys there are trained to remain three or four days under water, diving after the stones.

"Beyond the stone river are the ten tribes of the Jews, which, though subject to their own kings, are, for all that, our slaves and tributary to our Majesty. In one of our lands, hight Zone, are worms called in our tongue Salamanders. These worms can only live in fire, and they build cocoons like silk-worms, which are unwound by the ladies of our palace, and spun into cloth and dresses, which are worn by our Exaltedness. These dresses, in order to be cleaned and washed, are cast into flames.... When we go to war, we have fourteen golden and bejewelled crosses borne before us instead of banners; each of these crosses is followed by 10,000 horsemen, and 100,000 foot soldiers fully armed, without reckoning those in charge of the luggage and provision.

"When we ride abroad plainly, we have a wooden, unadorned cross, without gold or gem about it, borne before us, in order that we may meditate on the sufferings of Our Lord Jesus Christ; also a golden bowl filled with earth, to remind us of that whence we sprung, and that to which we must return; but besides these there is borne a silver bowl full of gold, as a token to all that we are the Lord of Lords.

"All riches, such as are upon the world, our Magnificence possesses in superabundance. With us no one lies, for he who speaks a lie is thenceforth regarded as dead; he is no more thought of, or honored by us. No vice is tolerated by us. Every year we undertake a pilgrimage, with retinue of war, to the body of the holy prophet Daniel, which is near the desolated site of Babylon. In our realm fishes are caught, the blood of which dyes purple. The Amazons and the Brahmins are subject to us. The palace in which our Supereminency resides, is built after the pattern of the castle built by the Apostle Thomas for the Indian king Gundoforus. Ceilings, joists, and architrave are of Sethym wood, the roof of ebony, which can never catch fire. Over the gable of the palace are, at the extremities, two golden apples, in each of which are two carbuncles, so that the gold may shine by day, and the carbuncles by night. The greater gates of the palace are of sardius, with the horn of the horned snake inwrought, so that no one can bring poison within.

"The other portals are of ebony. The windows are of crystal; the tables are partly of gold, partly of amethyst, and the columns supporting the tables are partly of ivory, partly of amethyst. The court in which we watch the jousting is floored with onyx in order to increase the courage of the combatants. In the palace, at night, nothing is burned for light but wicks supplied with balsam.... Before our palace stands a mirror, the ascent to which consists of five and twenty steps of porphyry and serpentine." After a description of the gems adorning this mirror, which is guarded night and day by three thousand armed men, he explains its use: "We look therein and behold all that is taking place in every province and region subject to our sceptre.

"Seven kings wait upon us monthly, in turn, with sixty-two dukes, two hundred and fifty-six counts and marquises: and twelve archbishops sit at table with us on our right, and twenty bishops on the left, besides the patriarch of St. Thomas, the Sarmatian Protopope, and the Archpope of Susa.... Our lord high steward is a primate and king, our cup-bearer is an archbishop and king, our chamberlain a bishop and king, our marshal a king and abbot."

I may be spared further extracts from this extraordinary letter, which proceeds to describe the church in which Prester John worships, by enumerating the precious stones of which it is constructed, and their special virtues.

Whether this letter was in circulation before Pope Alexander wrote his, it is not easy to decide. Alexander does not allude to it, but speaks of the reports which have reached him of the piety and the magnificence of the Priest-King. At the same time, there runs a tone of bitterness through the letter, as though the Pope had been galled at the pretensions of this mysterious personage, and perhaps winced under the prospect of the man-eaters overrunning Italy, as suggested by John the Priest. The papal epistle is an assertion of the claims of the See of Rome to universal dominion, and it assures the Eastern Prince-Pope that his Christian professions are worthless, unless he submits to the successor of Peter. "Not every one that saith unto me, Lord, Lord," &c., quotes the Pope, and then explains that the will of God is that every monarch and prelate should eat humble pie to the Sovereign Pontiff.

Sir John Maundevil gives the origin of the priestly title of the Eastern despot, in his curious book of travels.

"So it befelle, that this emperour cam, with a Cristene knyght with him, into a chirche in Egypt: and it was Saterday in Wyttson woke. And the bishop made orders. And he beheld and listened the servyse fulle tentyfly: and he asked the Cristene knyght, what men of degree thei scholden ben, that the prelate had before him. And the knyght answerede and seyde, that thei scholde ben prestes. And then the emperour seyde, that he wolde no longer ben clept kyng ne emperour, but preest: and that he wolde have the name of the first preest, that wente out of the chirche; and his name was John. And so evere more sittiens, he is clept Prestre John."

It is probable that the foundation of the whole Prester-John myth lay in the report which reached Europe of the wonderful successes of Nestorianism in the East, and there seems reason to believe that the famous letter given above was a Nestorian fabrication. It certainly looks un-European; the gorgeous imagery is thoroughly Eastern, and the disparaging tone in which Rome is spoken of could hardly have been the expression of Western feelings. The letter has the object in view of exalting the East in religion and arts to an undue eminence at the expense of the West, and it manifests some ignorance of European geography, when it speaks of the land extending from Spain to the Polar Sea. Moreover, the sites of the patriarchates, and the dignity conferred on that of St. Thomas, are indications of a Nestorian bias.

A brief glance at the history of this heretical Church may be of value here, as showing that there really was a foundation for the wild legends concerning a Christian empire in the East, so prevalent in Europe. Nestorius, a priest of Antioch and a disciple of St. Chrysostom, was elevated by the emperor to the patriarchate of Constantinople, and in the year 428 began to propagate his heresy, denying the hypostatic union. The Council of Ephesus denounced him, and, in spite of the emperor and court, Nestorius was anathematized and driven into exile. His sect spread through the

East, and became a flourishing church. It reached to China, where the emperor was all but converted; its missionaries traversed the frozen tundras of Siberia, preaching their maimed Gospel to the wild hordes which haunted those dreary wastes; it faced Buddhism, and wrestled with it for the religious supremacy in Thibet; it established churches in Persia and in Bokhara; it penetrated India; it formed colonies in Ceylon, in Siam, and in Sumatra; so that the Catholicos or Pope of Bagdad exercised sway more extensive than that ever obtained by the successor of St. Peter. The number of Christians belonging to that communion probably exceeded that of the members of the true Catholic Church in East and West. But the Nestorian Church was not founded on the Rock; it rested on Nestorius; and when the rain descended, and the winds blew, and the floods came, and beat upon that house, it fell, leaving scarce a fragment behind.

Rubruquis the Franciscan, who in 1253 was sent on a mission into Tartary, was the first to let in a little light on the fable. He writes, "The Catai dwelt beyond certain mountains across which I wandered, and in a plain in the midst of the mountains lived once an important Nestorian shepherd, who ruled over the Nestorian people, called Nayman. When Coir-Khan died, the Nestorian people raised this man to be king, and called him King Johannes, and related of him ten times as much as the truth. The Nestorians thereabouts have this way with them, that about nothing they make a great fuss, and thus they have got it noised abroad that Sartach, Mangu-Khan, and Ken-Khan were Christians, simply because they treated Christians well, and showed them more honor than other people. Yet, in fact, they were not Christians at all. And in like manner the story got about that there was a great King John. However, I traversed his pastures, and no one knew anything about him, except a few Nestorians. In his pastures lives Ken-Khan, at whose court was Brother Andrew, whom I met on my way back. This Johannes had a brother, a famous shepherd, named Unc, who lived three weeks' journey beyond the mountains of Caracatais."

This Unk-Khan was a real individual; he lost his life in the year 1203. Kuschhik, prince of the Nayman, and follower of Kor-Khan, fell in 1218.

Marco Polo, the Venetian traveller (1254-1324), identifies Unk-Khan with Prester John; he says, "I will now tell you of the deeds of the Tartars, how they gained the mastery, and spread over the whole earth. The Tartars dwelt between Georgia and Bargu, where there is a vast plain and level country, on which are neither cities nor forts, but capital pasturage and water. They had no chief of their own, but paid to Prester Johannes tribute. Of the greatness of this Prester Johannes, who was properly called Un-Khan, the whole world spake; the Tartars gave him one of every ten head of cattle. When Prester John noticed that they were increasing, he feared them, and planned how he could injure them. He determined therefore to scatter them, and he sent barons to do this. But the Tartars guessed what Prester John purposed ... and they went away into the wide wastes of the North, where they might be beyond his reach." He then goes on to relate how Tschengis-(Jenghiz-)Khan became the head of the Tartars, and how he fought against Prester John, and, after a desperate fight, overcame and slew him.

The Syriac Chronicle of the Jacobite Primate, Gregory Bar-Hebræus (born 1226, died 1286), also identifies Unk-Khan with Prester John. "In the year of the Greeks 1514, of the Arabs 599 (A. D. 1202), when Unk-Khan, who is the Christian King John, ruled over a stock of the barbarian Hunns, called Kergt, Tschingys-Khan served him with great zeal. When John observed the superiority and serviceableness of the other, he envied him, and plotted to seize and murder him. But two sons of Unk-Khan, having heard this, told it to Tschingys; whereupon he and his comrades fled by night, and secreted themselves. Next morning Unk-Khan took possession of the Tartar tents, but found them empty. Then the party of Tschingys fell upon him, and they met by the spring called Balschunah, and the side of Tschingys won the day; and the followers of Unk-Khan were compelled to yield. They met again several times, till Unk-Khan was utterly discomfited, and was slain himself, and his wives, sons, and daughters carried into captivity. Yet we must consider that King John the Kergtajer was not cast down for nought; nay, rather, because he had turned his heart from the fear of Christ his Lord, who had exalted him, and had taken a wife of the Zinish nation, called Quarakhata. Because he forsook the religion of his ancestors and followed strange gods, therefore God took the government from him, and gave it to one better than he, and whose heart was right before God."

Some of the early travellers, such as John de Plano Carpini and Marco Polo, in disabusing the popular mind of the belief in Prester John as a mighty Asiatic Christian monarch, unintentionally turned the popular faith in that individual into a new direction. They spoke of the black people of Abascia in Ethiopia, which, by the way, they called Middle India, as a great people subject to a Christian monarch.

Marco Polo says that the true monarch of Abyssinia is Christ; but that it is governed by six kings, three of whom are Christians and three Saracens, and that they are in league with the Soudan of Aden.

Bishop Jordanus, in his description of the world, accordingly sets down Abyssinia as the kingdom of Prester John; and such was the popular impression, which was confirmed by the appearance at intervals of ambassadors at European courts from the King of Abyssinia. The discovery of the Cape of Good Hope was due partly to a desire manifested in Portugal to open communications with this monarch,[22] and King John II. sent two men learned in Oriental languages through Egypt to the court of Abyssinia. The might and dominion of this prince, who had replaced the Tartar chief in the popular creed as Prester John, was of course greatly exaggerated, and was supposed to extend across Arabia and Asia to the wall of China. The spread of geographical knowledge has contracted the area of his dominions, and a critical acquaintance with history has exploded the myth which invested Unk-Khan, the nomad chief, with all the attributes of a demigod, uniting in one the utmost pretensions of a Pope and the proudest claims of a monarch.

---

[22] Ludolfi Hist. Æthiopica, lib. ii. cap. 1, 2. Petrus, Petri filius Lusitaniæ princeps, M. Pauli Veneti librum (qui de Indorum rebus multa: speciatim vero de Presbytero Johanne aliqua magnifice scripsit) Venetiis secum in patriam detulerat, qui (Chronologicis Lusitanorum testantibus) præcipuam Johanni Regi ansam dedit Indicæ navigationis, quam Henricus Johannis I. filius, patruus ejus, tentaverat, prosequendæ, &c.

THE DIVINING ROD

FROM the remotest period a rod has been regarded as the symbol of power and authority, and Holy Scripture employs it in the popular sense. Thus David speaks of "Thy rod and Thy staff comforting me;" and Moses works his miracles before Pharaoh with the rod as emblem of Divine commission. It was his rod which became a serpent, which turned the water of Egypt into blood, which opened the waves of the Red Sea and restored them to their former level, which "smote the rock of stone so that the water gushed out abundantly." The rod of Aaron acted an oracular part in the contest with the princes; laid up before the ark, it budded and brought forth almonds. In this instance we have it no longer as a symbol of authority, but as a means of divining the will of God. And as such it became liable to abuse; thus Hosea rebukes the chosen people for practising similar divinations. "My people ask counsel at their stocks, and their staff declareth unto them."[23]

Long before this, Jacob had made a different use of rods, employing them as a charm to make his father-in-law's sheep bear pied and spotted lambs.

We find rhabdomancy a popular form of divination among the Greeks, and also among the Romans. Cicero in his "De Officiis" alludes to it. "If all that is needful for our nourishment and support arrives to us by means of some divine rod, as people say, then each of us, free from all care and trouble, may give himself up to the exclusive pursuit of study and science."

Probably it is to this rod that the allusion of Ennius, as the agent in discovering hidden treasures, quoted in the first book of his "De Divinatione," refers.

According to Vetranius Maurus, Varro left a satire on the "Virgula divina," which has not been preserved. Tacitus tells us that the Germans practised some sort of divination by means of

---

[23] Hos. iv. 12.

rods. "For the purpose their method is simple. They cut a rod off some fruit-tree into bits, and after having distinguished them by various marks, they cast them into a white cloth.... Then the priest thrice draws each piece, and explains the oracle according to the marks." Ammianus Marcellinus says that the Alains employed an osier rod.

The fourteenth law of the Frisons ordered that the discovery of murders should be made by means of divining rods used in Church. These rods should be laid before the altar, and on the sacred relics, after which God was to be supplicated to indicate the culprit. This was called the Lot of Rods, or Tan-teen, the Rod of Rods.

But the middle ages was the date of the full development of the superstition, and the divining rod was believed to have efficacy in discovering hidden treasures, veins of precious metal, springs of water, thefts, and murders. The first notice of its general use among late writers is in the "Testamentum Novum," lib. i. cap. 25, of Basil Valentine, a Benedictine monk of the fifteenth century. Basil speaks of the general faith in and adoption of this valuable instrument for the discovery of metals, which is carried by workmen in mines, either in their belts or in their caps. He says that there are seven names by which this rod is known, and to its excellences under each title he devotes a chapter of his book. The names are: Divine Rod, Shining Rod, Leaping Rod, Transcendent Rod, Trembling Rod, Dipping Rod, Superior Rod. In his admirable treatise on metals, Agricola speaks of the rod in terms of disparagement; he considers its use as a relic of ancient magical forms, and he says that it is only irreligious workmen who employ it in their search after metals. Goclenius, however, in his treatise on the virtue of plants, stoutly does battle for the properties of the hazel rod. Whereupon Roberti, a Flemish Jesuit, falls upon him tooth and nail, disputes his facts, overwhelms him with abuse, and gibbets him for popular ridicule. Andreas Libavius, a writer I have already quoted in my article on the Wandering Jew, undertook a series of experiments upon the hazel divining rod, and concluded that there was truth in the popular belief. The Jesuit Kircher also "experimentalized several times on wooden rods which were declared to be sympathetic with regard to certain metals, by placing them on delicate pivots in equilibrium; but they never turned on the approach of metal." (De Arte Magnetica.) However, a similar course of experiments over water led him to attribute to the rod the power of indicating subterranean springs and water-courses; "I would not affirm it," he says, "unless I had established the fact by my own experience."

Dechales, another Jesuit, author of a treatise on natural springs, and of a huge tome entitled "Mundus Mathematicus," declared in the latter work, that no means of discovering sources is equal to the divining rod; and he quotes a friend of his who, with a hazel rod in his hand, could discover springs with the utmost precision and facility, and could trace on the surface of the ground the course of a subterranean conduit. Another writer, Saint-Romain, in his "Science dégagée des Chimères de l'École," exclaims, "Is it not astonishing to see a rod, which is held firmly in the hands, bow itself and turn visibly in the direction of water or metal, with more or less promptitude, according as the metal or the water are near or remote from the surface!"

In 1659 the Jesuit Gaspard Schott writes that the rod is used in every town of Germany, and that he had frequent opportunity of seeing it used in the discovery of hidden treasures. "I searched with the greatest care," he adds, "into the question whether the hazel rod had any sympathy with gold and silver, and whether any natural property set it in motion. In like manner I tried whether a ring of metal, held suspended by a thread in the midst of a tumbler, and which strikes the hours, is moved by any similar force. I ascertained that these effects could only have rise from the deception of those holding the rod or the pendulum, or, may be, from some diabolic impulsion, or, more likely still, because imagination sets the hand in motion."

The Sieur le Royer, a lawyer of Rouen, in 1674, published his "Traité du Bâton universel," in which he gives an account of a trial made with the rod in the presence of Father Jean François, who had ridiculed the operation in his treatise on the science of waters, published at Rennes in 1655, and which succeeded in convincing the blasphemer of the divine Rod. Le Royer denies to it the power of picking out criminals, which had been popularly attributed to it, and as had been unhesitatingly claimed for it by Debrio in his "Disquisitio Magica."

And now I am brought to the extraordinary story of Jacques Aymar, which attracted the attention of Europe to the marvellous properties of the divining rod. I shall give the history of this man in full, as such an account is rendered necessary by the mutilated versions I have seen current in English magazine articles, which follow the lead of Mrs. Crowe, who narrates the earlier portion of this impostor's career, but says nothing of his exposé and downfall.

On the 5th July, 1692, at about ten o'clock in the evening, a wine-seller of Lyons and his wife were assassinated in their cellar, and their money carried off. On the morrow, the officers of justice arrived, and examined the premises. Beside the corpses, lay a large bottle wrapped in straw, and a bloody hedging bill, which undoubtedly had been the instrument used to accomplish the murder. Not a trace of those who had committed the horrible deed was to be found, and the magistrates were quite at fault as to the direction in which they should turn for a clew to the murderer or murderers.

At this juncture a neighbor reminded the magistrates of an incident which had taken place four years previous. It was this. In 1688 a theft of clothes had been made in Grenoble. In the parish of Crôle lived a man named Jacques Aymar, supposed to be endowed with the faculty of using the divining rod. This man was sent for. On reaching the spot where the theft had been committed, his rod moved in his hand. He followed the track indicated by the rod, and it continued to rotate between his fingers as long as he followed a certain direction, but ceased to turn if he diverged from it in the smallest degree. Guided by his rod, Aymar went from street to street, till he was brought to a standstill before the prison gates. These could not be opened without leave of the magistrate, who hastened to witness the experiment. The gates were unlocked, and Aymar, under the same guidance, directed his steps towards four prisoners lately incarcerated. He ordered the four to be stood in a line, and then he placed his foot on that of the first. The rod remained immovable. He passed to the second, and the rod turned at once. Before the third prisoner there were no signs; the fourth trembled, and begged to be heard. He owned himself the thief, along with the second, who also acknowledged the theft, and mentioned the name of the receiver of the stolen goods. This was a farmer in the neighborhood of Grenoble. The magistrate and officers visited him and demanded the articles he had obtained. The farmer denied all knowledge of the theft and all participation in the booty. Aymar, however, by means of his rod, discovered the secreted property, and restored it to the persons from whom it had been stolen.

On another occasion Aymar had been in quest of a spring of water, when he felt his rod turn sharply in his hand. On digging at the spot, expecting to discover an abundant source, the body of a murdered woman was found in a barrel, with a rope twisted round her neck. The poor creature was recognized as a woman of the neighborhood who had vanished four months before. Aymar went to the house which the victim had inhabited, and presented his rod to each member of the household. It turned upon the husband of the deceased, who at once took to flight.

The magistrates of Lyons, at their wits' ends how to discover the perpetrators of the double murder in the wine shop, urged the Procureur du Roi to make experiment of the powers of Jacques Aymar. The fellow was sent for, and he boldly asserted his capacity for detecting criminals, if he were first brought to the spot of the murder, so as to be put en rapport with the murderers.

He was at once conducted to the scene of the outrage, with the rod in his hand. This remained stationary as he traversed the cellar, till he reached the spot where the body of the wine seller had lain; then the stick became violently agitated, and the man's pulse rose as though he were in an access of fever. The same motions and symptoms manifested themselves when he reached the place where the second victim had lain.

Having thus received his impression, Aymar left the cellar, and, guided by his rod, or rather by an internal instinct, he ascended into the shop, and then stepping into the street, he followed from one to another, like a hound upon the scent, the track of the murderers. It conducted him into the court of the archiepiscopal palace, across it, and down to the gate of the Rhone. It was now evening, and the city gates being all closed, the quest of blood was relinquished for the night.

Next morning Aymar returned to the scent. Accompanied by three officers, he left the gate, and descended the right bank of the Rhone. The rod gave indications of there having been three involved in the murder, and he pursued the traces till two of them led to a gardener's cottage. Into this he entered, and there he asserted with warmth, against the asseverations of the proprietor to the contrary, that the fugitives had entered his room, had seated themselves at his table, and had drunk wine out of one of the bottles which he indicated. Aymar tested each of the household with his rod, to see if they had been in contact with the murderers. The rod moved over the two children only, aged respectively ten and nine years. These little things, on being questioned, answered, with reluctance, that during their father's absence on Sunday morning, against his express commands, they had left the door open, and that two men, whom they described, had come in suddenly upon them, and had seated themselves and made free with the wine in the bottle pointed out by the man with the rod. This first verification of the talents of Jacques Aymar convinced some of the sceptical, but the Procurateur Général forbade the prosecution of the experiment till the man had been further tested.

As already stated, a hedging bill had been discovered, on the scene of the murder, smeared with blood, and unquestionably the weapon with which the crime had been committed. Three bills from the same maker, and of precisely the same description, were obtained, and the four were taken into a garden, and secretly buried at intervals. Aymar was then brought, staff in hand, into the garden, and conducted over the spots where lay the bills. The rod began to vibrate as his feet stood upon the place where was concealed the bill which had been used by the assassins, but was motionless elsewhere. Still unsatisfied, the four bills were exhumed and concealed anew. The comptroller of the province himself bandaged the sorcerer's eyes, and led him by the hand from place to place. The divining rod showed no signs of movement till it approached the blood-stained weapon, when it began to oscillate.

The magistrates were now so far satisfied as to agree that Jacques Aymar should be authorized to follow the trail of the murderers, and have a company of archers to follow him.

Guided by his rod, Aymar now recommenced his pursuit. He continued tracing down the right bank of the Rhone till he came to half a league from the bridge of Lyons. Here the footprints of three men were observed in the sand, as though engaged in entering a boat. A rowing boat was obtained, and Aymar, with his escort, descended the river; he found some difficulty in following the trail upon water; still he was able, with a little care, to detect it. It brought him under an arch of the bridge of Vienne, which boats rarely passed beneath. This proved that the fugitives were without a guide. The way in which this curious journey was made was singular. At intervals Aymar was put ashore to test the banks with his rod, and ascertain whether the murderers had landed. He discovered the places where they had slept, and indicated the chairs or benches on which they had sat. In this manner, by slow degrees, he arrived at the military camp of Sablon, between Vienne and Saint-Valier. There Aymar felt violent agitation, his cheeks flushed, and his pulse beat with rapidity. He penetrated the crowds of soldiers, but did not venture to use his rod, lest the men should take it ill, and fall upon him. He could not do more without special authority, and was constrained to return to Lyons. The magistrates then provided him with the requisite powers, and he went back to the camp. Now he declared that the murderers were not there. He recommenced his pursuit, and descended the Rhone again as far as Beaucaire.

On entering the town he ascertained by means of his rod that those whom he was pursuing had parted company. He traversed several streets, then crowded on account of the annual fair, and was brought to a standstill before the prison doors. One of the murderers was within, he declared; he would track the others afterwards. Having obtained permission to enter, he was brought into the presence of fourteen or fifteen prisoners. Amongst these was a hunchback, who had only an hour previously been incarcerated on account of a theft he had committed at the fair. Aymar applied his rod to each of the prisoners in succession: it turned upon the hunchback. The sorcerer ascertained that the other two had left the town by a little path leading into the Nismes road. Instead of following this track, he returned to Lyons with the hunchback and the guard. At Lyons a triumph awaited him. The hunchback had hitherto protested his innocence, and declared that he had never set foot in Lyons. But as he was brought to that town by the way along which Aymar had ascertained that he had left it, the fellow was recognized at the different houses where he had lodged the night, or stopped for food. At the little town of Bagnols, he was confronted with the host and hostess of a tavern where he and his comrades had slept, and they swore to his identity, and accurately described his companions: their description tallied with that given by the children of the gardener. The wretched man was so confounded by this recognition, that he avowed having staid there, a few days before, along with two Provençals. These men, he said, were the criminals; he had been their servant, and had only kept guard in the upper room whilst they committed the murders in the cellar.

On his arrival in Lyons he was committed to prison, and his trial was decided on. At his first interrogation he told his tale precisely as he had related it before, with these additions: the murderers spoke patois, and had purchased two bills. At ten o'clock in the evening all three had entered the wine shop. The Provençals had a large bottle wrapped in straw, and they persuaded the publican and his wife to descend with them into the cellar to fill it, whilst he, the hunchback, acted as watch in the shop. The two men murdered the wine-seller and his wife with their bills, and then mounted to the shop, where they opened the coffer, and stole from it one hundred and thirty crowns, eight louis-d'ors, and a silver belt. The crime accomplished, they took refuge in the court of a large house,—this was the archbishop's palace, indicated by

Aymar,—and passed the night in it. Next day, early, they left Lyons, and only stopped for a moment at a gardener's cottage. Some way down the river, they found a boat moored to the bank. This they loosed from its mooring and entered. They came ashore at the spot pointed out by the man with the stick. They staid some days in the camp at Sablon, and then went on to Beaucaire.

Aymar was now sent in quest of the other murderers. He resumed their trail at the gate of Beaucaire, and that of one of them, after considerable détours, led him to the prison doors of Beaucaire, and he asked to be allowed to search among the prisoners for his man. This time he was mistaken. The second fugitive was not within; but the jailer affirmed that a man whom he described—and his description tallied with the known appearance of one of the Provençals—had called at the gate shortly after the removal of the hunchback to inquire after him, and on learning of his removal to Lyons, had hurried off precipitately. Aymar now followed his track from the prison, and this brought him to that of the third criminal. He pursued the double scent for some days. But it became evident that the two culprits had been alarmed at what had transpired in Beaucaire, and were flying from France. Aymar traced them to the frontier, and then returned to Lyons.

On the 30th of August, 1692, the poor hunchback was, according to sentence, broken on the wheel, in the Place des Terreaux. On his way to execution he had to pass the wine shop. There the recorder publicly read his sentence, which had been delivered by thirty judges. The criminal knelt and asked pardon of the poor wretches in whose murder he was involved, after which he continued his course to the place fixed for his execution.

It may be well here to give an account of the authorities for this extraordinary story. There are three circumstantial accounts, and numerous letters written by the magistrate who sat during the trial, and by an eye-witness of the whole transaction, men honorable and disinterested, upon whose veracity not a shadow of doubt was supposed to rest by their contemporaries.

M. Chauvin, Doctor of Medicine, published a "Lettre à Mme. la Marquise de Senozan, sur les moyens dont on s'est servi pour découvrir les complices d'un assassinat commis à Lyon, le 5 Juillet, 1692." Lyons, 1692. The procès-verbal of the Procureur du Roi, M. de Vanini, is also extant, and published in the Physique occulte of the Abbé de Vallemont.

Pierre Gamier, Doctor of Medicine of the University of Montpellier, wrote a Dissertation physique en forme de lettre, à M. de Sève, seigneur de Fléchères, on Jacques Aymar, printed the same year at Lyons, and republished in the Histoire critique des pratiques superstitieuses du Père Lebrun.

Doctor Chauvin was witness of nearly all the circumstances related, as was also the Abbé Lagarde, who has written a careful account of the whole transaction as far as to the execution of the hunchback.

Another eye-witness writes to the Abbé Bignon a letter printed by Lebrun in his Histoire critique cited above. "The following circumstance happened to me yesterday evening," he says: "M. le Procureur du Roi here, who, by the way, is one of the wisest and cleverest men in the country, sent for me at six o'clock, and had me conducted to the scene of the murder. We found there M. Grimaut, director of the customs, whom I knew to be a very upright man, and a young attorney named Besson, with whom I am not acquainted, but who M. le Procureur du Roi told me had the power of using the rod as well as M. Grimaut. We descended into the cellar where the murder had been committed, and where there were still traces of blood. Each time that M. Grimaut and the attorney passed the spot where the murder had been perpetrated, the rods they held in their hands began to turn, but ceased when they stepped beyond the spot. We tried experiments for more than an hour, as also with the bill, which M. le Procureur had brought along with him, and they were satisfactory. I observed several curious facts in the attorney. The rod in his hands was more violently moved than in those of M. Grimaut, and when I placed one of my fingers in each of his hands, whilst the rod turned, I felt the most extraordinary throbbings of the arteries in his palms. His pulse was at fever heat. He sweated profusely, and at intervals he was compelled to go into the court to obtain fresh air."

The Sieur Pauthot, Dean of the College of Medicine at Lyons, gave his observations to the public as well. Some of them are as follows: "We began at the cellar in which the murder had been committed; into this the man with the rod (Aymar) shrank from entering, because he felt violent agitations which overcame him when he used the stick over the place where the corpses of those who had been assassinated had lain. On entering the cellar, the rod was put in my hands, and arranged by the master as most suitable for operation; I passed and repassed over the spot where the bodies had been found, but it remained immovable, and I felt no agitation. A lady of rank and merit, who was with us, took the rod after me; she felt it begin to move, and was internally agitated. Then the owner of the rod resumed it, and, passing over the same places, the stick rotated with such violence that it seemed easier to break than to stop it. The peasant then quitted our company to faint away, as was his wont after similar experiments. I followed him. He turned very pale and broke into a profuse perspiration, whilst for a quarter of an hour his pulse was violently troubled; indeed, the faintness was so considerable, that they were obliged to dash water in his face and give him water to drink in order to bring him round." He then describes experiments made over the bloody bill and others similar, which succeeded in the hands of Aymar and the lady, but failed when he attempted them himself. Pierre Garnier, physician of the medical college of Montpellier, appointed to that of Lyons, has also written an account of what he saw, as mentioned above. He gives a curious proof of Aymar's powers.

"M. le Lieutenant-Général having been robbed by one of his lackeys, seven or eight months ago, and having lost by him twenty-five crowns which had been taken out of one of the cabinets behind his library, sent for Aymar, and asked him to discover the circumstances. Aymar went several times round the chamber, rod in hand, placing one foot on the chairs, on the various articles of furniture, and on two bureaux which are in the apartment, each of which contains several drawers. He fixed on the very bureau and the identical drawer out of which the money had been stolen. M. le Lieutenant-Général bade him follow the track of the robber. He did so. With his rod he went out on a new terrace, upon which the cabinet opens, thence back into the cabinet and up to the fire, then into the library, and from thence he went direct up stairs to the lackeys' sleeping apartment, when the rod guided him to one of the beds, and turned over one side of the bed, remaining motionless over the other. The lackeys then present cried out that the thief had slept on the side indicated by the rod, the bed having been shared with another footman, who occupied the further side." Garnier gives a lengthy account of various experiments he made along with the Lieutenant-Général, the uncle of the same, the Abbé de St. Remain, and M. de Puget, to detect whether there was imposture in the man. But all their attempts failed to discover a trace of deception. He gives a report of a verbal examination of Aymar which is interesting. The man always replied with candor.

The report of the extraordinary discovery of murder made by the divining rod at Lyons attracted the attention of Paris, and Aymar was ordered up to the capital. There, however, his powers left him. The Prince de Condé submitted him to various tests, and he broke down under every one. Five holes were dug in the garden. In one was secreted gold, in another silver, in a third silver and gold, in the fourth copper, and in the fifth stones. The rod made no signs in presence of the metals, and at last actually began to move over the buried pebbles. He was sent to Chantilly to discover the perpetrators of a theft of trout made in the ponds of the park. He went round the water, rod in hand, and it turned at spots where he said the fish had been drawn out. Then, following the track of the thief, it led him to the cottage of one of the keepers, but did not move over any of the individuals then in the house. The keeper himself was absent, but arrived late at night, and, on hearing what was said, he roused Aymar from his bed, insisting on having his innocence vindicated. The divining rod, however, pronounced him guilty, and the poor fellow took to his heels, much upon the principle recommended by Montesquieu a while after. Said he, "If you are accused of having stolen the towers of Notre-Dame, bolt at once."

A peasant, taken at haphazard from the street, was brought to the sorcerer as one suspected. The rod turned slightly, and Aymar declared that the man did not steal the fish, but ate of them. A boy was then introduced, who was said to be the keeper's son. The rod rotated violently at once. This was the finishing stroke, and Aymar was sent away by the Prince in disgrace. It now transpired that the theft of fish had taken place seven years before, and the lad was no relation of the keeper, but a country boy who had only been in Chantilly eight or ten months. M. Goyonnot, Recorder of the King's Council, broke a window in his house, and sent for the diviner, to whom he related a story of his having been robbed of valuables during the night. Aymar indicated the broken window as the means whereby the thief had entered the house, and pointed out the window by which he had left it with the booty. As no such robbery had been committed, Aymar was turned out of the house as an impostor. A few similar cases brought him into such disrepute that he was obliged to leave Paris, and return to Grenoble.

Some years after, he was made use of by the Maréchal Montrevel, in his cruel pursuit of the Camisards.

Was Aymar an impostor from first to last, or did his powers fail him in Paris? and was it only then that he had recourse to fraud?

Much may be said in favor of either supposition. His exposé at Paris tells heavily against him, but need not be regarded as conclusive evidence of imposture throughout his career. If he really did possess the powers he claimed, it is not to be supposed that these existed in full vigor under all conditions; and Paris is a place most unsuitable for testing them, built on artificial soil, and full of disturbing influences of every description. It has been remarked with others who used the rod, that their powers languished under excitement, and that the faculties had to be in repose, the attention to be concentrated on the subject of inquiry, or the action—nervous, magnetic, or electrical, or what you will—was impeded.

Now, Paris, visited for the first time by a poor peasant, its salons open to him, dazzling him with their splendor, and the novelty of finding himself in the midst of princes, dukes, marquises, and their families, not only may have agitated the countryman to such an extent as to deprive him of his peculiar faculty, but may have led him into simulating what he felt had departed from him, at the moment when he was under the eyes of the grandees of the Court. We have analogous cases in Bleton and Angelique Cottin. The former was a hydroscope, who fell into convulsions whenever he passed over running water. This peculiarity was noticed in him when a child of seven years old. When brought to Paris, he failed signally to detect the presence of water conveyed underground by pipes and conduits, but he pretended to feel the influence of water where there certainly was none. Angelique Cottin was a poor girl, highly charged with electricity. Any one touching her received a violent shock; one medical gentleman, having seated her on his knee, was knocked clean out of his chair by the electric fluid, which thus exhibited its sense of propriety. But the electric condition of Angelique became feebler as she approached Paris, and failed her altogether in the capital.

I believe that the imagination is the principal motive force in those who use the divining rod; but whether it is so solely, I am unable to decide. The powers of nature are so mysterious and inscrutable that we must be cautious in limiting them, under abnormal conditions, to the ordinary laws of experience.

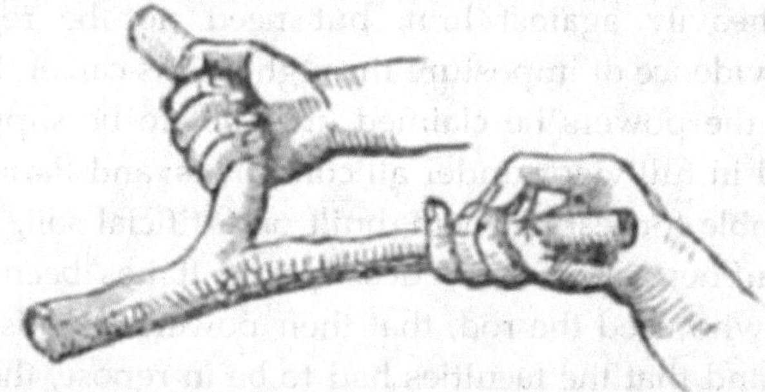

The manner in which the rod was used by certain persons renders self-deception possible. The rod is generally of hazel, and is forked like a Y; the forefingers are placed against the diverging arms of the rod, and the elbows are brought back against the side; thus the implement is held in front of the operator, delicately balanced before the pit of the stomach at a distance of about eight inches. Now, if the pressure of the balls of the digits be in the least relaxed, the stalk of the rod will naturally fall. It has been assumed by some, that a restoration of the pressure will bring the stem up again, pointing towards the operator, and a little further pressure will elevate it into a perpendicular position. A relaxation of force will again lower it, and thus the rotation observed in the rod be maintained. I confess myself unable to accomplish this. The lowering of the leg of the rod is easy enough, but no efforts of mine to produce a revolution on its axis have as yet succeeded. The muscles which would contract the fingers upon the arms of the stick, pass the shoulder; and it is worthy of remark that one of the medical men who witnessed the experiments made on Bleton the hydroscope, expressly alludes to a slight rising of the shoulders during the rotation of the divining rod.

But the manner of using the rod was by no means identical in all cases. If, in all cases, it had simply been balanced between the fingers, some probability might be given to the suggestion above made, that the rotation was always effected by the involuntary action of the muscles.

The usual manner of holding the rod, however, precluded such a possibility. The most ordinary use consisted in taking a forked stick in such a manner that the palms were turned upwards, and the fingers closed upon the branching arms of the rod. Some required the normal position of the rod to be horizontal, others elevated the point, others again depressed it.

If the implement were straight, it was held in a similar manner, but the hands were brought somewhat together, so as to produce a slight arc in the rod. Some who practised rhabdomancy sustained this species of rod between their thumbs and forefingers; or else the thumb and forefingers were closed, and the rod rested on their points; or again it reposed on the flat of the hand, or on the back, the hand being held vertically and the rod held in equilibrium.

A third species of divining rod consisted in a straight staff cut in two: one extremity of the one half was hollowed out, the other half was sharpened at the end, and this end was inserted in the hollow, and the pointed stick rotated in the cavity.

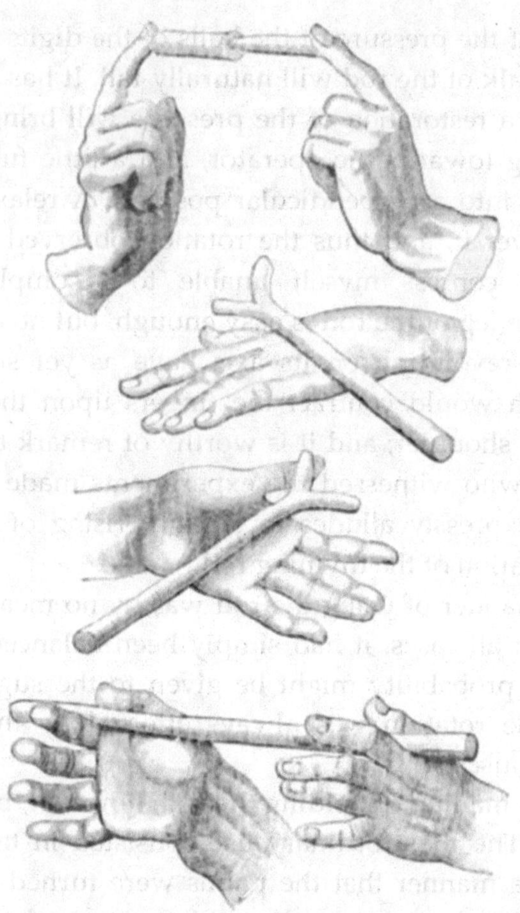

POSITIONS OF THE HANDS

From "Lettres qui découvrent l'Illusion des Philosophes sur la Baguette." Paris, 1693.

The way in which Bleton used his rod is thus minutely described: "He does not grasp it, nor warm it in his hands, and he does not regard with preference a hazel branch lately cut and full of sap. He places horizontally between his forefingers a rod of any kind given to him, or picked up in the road, of any sort of wood except elder, fresh or dry, not always forked, but sometimes merely bent. If it is straight, it rises slightly at the extremities by little jerks, but does not turn. If bent, it revolves on its axis with more or less rapidity, in more or less time, according to the quantity and current of the water. I counted from thirty to thirty-five revolutions in a minute, and afterwards as many as eighty. A curious phenomenon is, that Bleton is able to make the rod turn between another person's fingers, even without seeing it or touching it, by approaching his body towards it when his feet stand over a subterranean watercourse. It is true, however, that the motion is much less strong and less durable in other fingers than his own. If Bleton stood on his head, and placed the rod between his feet, though he felt strongly the peculiar sensations produced in him by flowing water, yet the rod remained stationary. If he were insulated on glass, silk, or wax, the sensations were less vivid, and the rotation of the stick ceased."

But this experiment failed in Paris, under circumstances which either proved that Bleton's imagination produced the movement, or that his integrity was questionable. It is quite possible that in many instances the action of the muscles is purely involuntary, and is attributable to the imagination, so that the operator deceives himself as well as others.

This is probably the explanation of the story of Mdlle. Olivet, a young lady of tender conscience, who was a skilful performer with the divining rod, but shrank from putting her powers in operation, lest she should be indulging in unlawful acts. She consulted the Père Lebrun, author of a work already referred to in this paper, and he advised her to ask God to withdraw the power from her, if the exercise of it was harmful to her spiritual condition. She entered into retreat for two days, and prayed with fervor. Then she made her communion, asking God what had been recommended to her at the moment when she received the Host. In the afternoon of the same day she made experiment with her rod, and found that it would no longer operate. The girl had strong faith in it before—a faith coupled with fear; and as long as that faith was strong in her, the rod moved; now she believed that the faculty was taken from her; and the power ceased with the loss of her faith.

If the divining rod is put in motion by any other force except the involuntary action of the muscles, we must confine its powers to the property of indicating the presence of flowing water. There are numerous instances of hydroscopes thus detecting the existence of a spring, or of a subterranean watercourse; the most remarkably endowed individuals of this description are Jean-Jacques Parangue, born near Marseilles, in 1760, who experienced a horror when near water which no one else perceived. He was endowed with the faculty of seeing water through the ground, says l'Abbé Sauri, who gives his history. Jenny Leslie, a Scotch girl, about the same date claimed similar powers. In 1790, Pennet, a native of Dauphiné, attracted attention in Italy, but when carefully tested by scientific men in Padua, his attempts to discover buried metals failed; at Florence he was detected in an endeavor to find out by night what had been secreted to test his powers on the morrow. Vincent Amoretti was an Italian, who underwent peculiar sensations when brought in proximity to water, coal, and salt; he was skilful in the use of the rod, but made no public exhibition of his powers.

The rod is still employed, I have heard it asserted, by Cornish miners; but I have never been able to ascertain that such is really the case. The mining captains whom I have questioned invariably repudiated all knowledge of its use.

In Wiltshire, however, it is still employed for the purpose of detecting water; and the following extract from a letter I have just received will show that it is still in vogue on the Continent:—

"I believe the use of the divining rod for discovering springs of water has by no means been confined to mediæval times; for I was personally acquainted with a lady, now deceased, who has successfully practised with it in this way. She was a very clever and accomplished woman; Scotch by birth and education; by no means credulous; possibly a a little imaginative, for she wrote not unsuccessfully; and of a remarkably open and straightforward disposition. Captain C——, her husband, had a large estate in Holstein, near Lubeck, supporting a considerable population; and whether for the wants of the people or for the improvement of the land, it now and then happened that an additional well was needed.

"On one of these occasions a man was sent for who made a

regular profession of finding water by the divining rod; there happened to be a large party staying at the house, and the whole company turned out to see the fun. The rod gave indications in the usual way, and water was ultimately found at the spot. Mrs. C——, utterly sceptical, took the rod into her own hands to make experiment, believing that she would prove the man an impostor; and she said afterwards she was never more frightened in her life than when it began to move, on her walking over the spring. Several other gentlemen and ladies tried it, but it was quite inactive in their hands. 'Well,' said the host to his wife, 'we shall have no occasion to send for the man again, as you are such an adept.'

"Some months after this, water was wanted in another part of the estate, and it occurred to Mrs. C—— that she would use the rod again. After some trials, it again gave decided indications, and a well was begun and carried down a very considerable depth. At last she began to shrink from incurring more expense, but the laborers had implicit faith; and begged to be allowed to persevere. Very soon the water burst up with such force that the men escaped with difficulty; and this proved afterwards the most unfailing spring for miles round.

"You will take the above for what it is worth; the facts I have given are undoubtedly true, whatever conclusions may be drawn from them. I do not propose that you should print my narrative, but I think in these cases personal testimony, even indirect, is more useful in forming one's opinion than a hundred old volumes. I did not hear it from Mrs. C——'s own lips, but I was sufficiently acquainted with her to form a very tolerable estimate of her character; and my wife, who has known her intimately from her own childhood, was in her younger days often staying with her for months together."

I remember having been much perplexed by reading a series of experiments made with a pendulous ring over metals, by a Mr. Mayo: he ascertained that it oscillated in various directions under peculiar circumstances, when suspended by a thread over the ball of the thumb. I instituted a series of experiments, and was surprised to find the ring vibrate in an unaccountable manner in opposite directions over different metals. On consideration, I closed my eyes whilst the ring was oscillating over gold, and on opening them I found that it had become stationary. I got a friend to change the metals whilst I was blindfolded—the ring no longer vibrated. I was thus enabled to judge of the involuntary action of muscles, quite sufficient to have deceived an eminent medical man like Mr. Mayo, and to have perplexed me till I succeeded in solving the mystery.[24]

<hr>

[24] A similar series of experiments was undertaken, as I learned afterwards, by M. Chevreuil in Paris, with similar results.

THE SEVEN SLEEPERS OF EPHESUS

ONE of the most picturesque myths of ancient days is that which forms the subject of this article. It is thus told by Jacques de Voragine, in his "Legenda Aurea:"—

"The seven sleepers were natives of Ephesus. The Emperor Decius, who persecuted the Christians, having come to Ephesus, ordered the erection of temples in the city, that all might come and sacrifice before him; and he commanded that the Christians should be sought out and given their choice, either to worship the idols, or to die. So great was the consternation in the city, that the friend denounced his friend, the father his son, and the son his father.

"Now there were in Ephesus seven Christians, Maximian, Malchus, Marcian, Dionysius, John, Serapion, and Constantine by name. These refused to sacrifice to the idols, and remained in their houses praying and fasting. They were accused before Decius, and they confessed themselves to be Christians. However, the emperor gave them a little time to consider what line they would adopt. They took advantage of this reprieve to dispense their goods among the poor, and then they retired, all seven, to Mount Celion, where they determined to conceal themselves.

"One of their number, Malchus, in the disguise of a physician, went to the town to obtain victuals. Decius, who had been absent from Ephesus for a little while, returned, and gave orders for the seven to be sought. Malchus, having escaped from the town, fled, full of fear, to his comrades, and told them of the emperor's fury. They were much alarmed; and Malchus handed them the loaves he had bought, bidding them eat, that, fortified by the food, they might have courage in the time of trial. They ate, and then, as they sat weeping and speaking to one another, by the will of God they fell asleep.

"The pagans sought everywhere, but could not find them, and Decius was greatly irritated at their escape. He had their parents brought before him, and threatened them with death if they did not reveal the place of concealment; but they could only answer that the seven young men had distributed their goods to the poor, and that they were quite ignorant as to their whereabouts.

"Decius, thinking it possible that they might be hiding in a cavern, blocked up the mouth with stones, that they might perish of hunger.

"Three hundred and sixty years passed, and in the thirtieth year of the reign of Theodosius, there broke forth a heresy denying the resurrection of the dead....

"Now, it happened that an Ephesian was building a stable on the side of Mount Celion, and finding a pile of stones handy, he took them for his edifice, and thus opened the mouth of the cave. Then the seven sleepers awoke, and it was to them as if they had slept but a single night. They began to ask Malchus what decision Decius had given concerning them.

"'He is going to hunt us down, so as to force us to sacrifice to the idols,' was his reply. 'God knows,' replied Maximian, 'we shall never do that.' Then exhorting his companions, he urged Malchus to go back to the town to buy some more bread, and at the same time to obtain fresh information. Malchus took five coins and left the cavern. On seeing the stones he was filled with astonishment; however, he went on towards the city; but what was his bewilderment, on approaching the gate, to see over it a cross! He went to another gate, and there he beheld the same sacred sign; and so he observed it over each gate of the city. He believed that he was suffering from the effects of a dream. Then he entered Ephesus, rubbing his eyes, and he walked to a baker's shop. He heard people using our Lord's name, and he was the more perplexed. 'Yesterday, no one dared pronounce the name of Jesus, and now it is on every one's lips. Wonderful! I can hardly believe myself to be in Ephesus.' He asked a passer-by the name of the city, and on being told it was Ephesus, he was thunderstruck. Now he entered a baker's shop, and laid down his money. The baker, examining the coin, inquired whether he had found a treasure, and began to whisper to some others in the shop. The youth, thinking that he was discovered, and that they were about to conduct him to the emperor, implored them to let him alone, offering to leave loaves and money if he might only be suffered to escape. But the shop-men, seizing him, said, 'Whoever you are, you have found a treasure; show us where it is, that we may share it with you, and then we will hide you.' Malchus was too frightened to answer. So they put a rope round his neck, and drew him through the streets into the market-place. The news soon spread that the young man had discovered a great treasure, and there was presently a vast crowd about him. He stoutly protested his innocence. No one recognized him, and his eyes, ranging over the faces which surrounded him, could not see one which he had known, or which was in the slightest degree familiar to him.

"St. Martin, the bishop, and Antipater, the governor, having heard of the excitement, ordered the young man to be brought before them, along with the bakers.

"The bishop and the governor asked him where he had found the treasure, and he replied that he had found none, but that the few coins were from his own purse. He was next asked whence he came. He replied that he was a native of Ephesus, 'if this be Ephesus.'

"'Send for your relations—your parents, if they live here,' ordered the governor.

"'They live here, certainly,' replied the youth; and he mentioned their names. No such names were known in the town. Then the governor exclaimed, 'How dare you say that this money belonged to your parents when it dates back three hundred and seventy-seven years,[25] and is as old as the beginning of the reign of Decius, and it is utterly unlike our modern coinage? Do you think to impose on the old men and sages of Ephesus? Believe me, I shall make you suffer the severities of the law till you show where you made the discovery.'

"'I implore you,' cried Malchus, 'in the name of God, answer me a few questions, and then I will answer yours. Where is the Emperor Decius gone to?'

"The bishop answered, 'My son, there is no emperor of that name; he who was thus called died long ago.'

"Malchus replied, 'All I hear perplexes me more and more. Follow me, and I will show you my comrades, who fled with me into a cave of Mount Celion, only yesterday, to escape the cruelty of Decius. I will lead you to them.'

"The bishop turned to the governor. 'The hand of God is here,' he said. Then they followed, and a great crowd after them. And Malchus entered first into the cavern to his companions, and the bishop after him.... And there they saw the martyrs seated in the cave, with their faces fresh and blooming as roses; so all fell down and glorified God. The bishop and the governor sent notice to Theodosius, and he hurried to Ephesus. All the inhabitants met him and conducted him to the cavern. As soon as the saints beheld the emperor, their faces shone like the sun, and the emperor gave thanks unto God, and embraced them, and said, 'I see you, as though I saw the Savior restoring Lazarus.' Maximian replied, 'Believe us! for the faith's sake, God has resuscitated us before the great resurrection day, in order that you may believe firmly in the resurrection of the dead. For as the child is in its mother's womb living and not suffering, so have we lived without suffering, fast asleep.' And having thus spoken,

____

[25] This calculation is sadly inaccurate.

they bowed their heads, and their souls returned to their
Maker. The emperor, rising, bent over them and embraced
them weeping. He gave them orders for golden reliquaries
to be made, but that night they appeared to him in a
dream, and said that hitherto they had slept in the earth,
and that in the earth they desired to sleep on till God
should raise them again."

Such is the beautiful story. It seems to have travelled to us from
the East. Jacobus Sarugiensis, a Mesopotamian bishop, in the fifth
or sixth century, is said to have been the first to commit it to
writing. Gregory of Tours (De Glor. Mart. i. 9) was perhaps the first
to introduce it to Europe. Dionysius of Antioch (ninth century) told
the story in Syrian, and Photius of Constantinople reproduced it,
with the remark that Mahomet had adopted it into the Koran.
Metaphrastus alludes to it as well; in the tenth century Eutychius
inserted it in his annals of Arabia; it is found in the Coptic and the
Maronite books, and several early historians, as Paulus Diaconus,
Nicephorus, &c., have inserted it in their works.

A poem on the Seven Sleepers was composed by a trouvère
named Chardri, and is mentioned by M. Fr. Michel in his "Rapports
Ministre de l'Instruction Public;" a German poem on the same
subject, of the thirteenth century, in 935 verses, has been published
by M. Karajan; and the Spanish poet, Augustin Morreto, composed
a drama on it, entitled "Los Siete Durmientes," which is inserted in
the 19th volume of the rare work, "Comedias Nuevas Escogidas de
los Mejores Ingenios."

Mahomet has somewhat improved on the story. He has made
the Sleepers prophesy his coming, and he has given them a dog
named Kratim, or Kratimir, which sleeps with them, and which is
endowed with the gift of prophecy.

As a special favor this dog is to be one of the ten animals to be
admitted into his paradise, the others being Jonah's whale,
Solomon's ant, Ishmael's ram, Abraham's calf, the Queen of Sheba's
ass, the prophet Salech's camel, Moses' ox, Belkis' cuckoo, and
Mahomet's ass.

It was perhaps too much for the Seven Sleepers to ask, that

their bodies should be left to rest in earth. In ages when saintly relics were valued above gold and precious stones, their request was sure to be shelved; and so we find that their remains were conveyed to Marseilles in a large stone sarcophagus, which is still exhibited in St. Victor's Church. In the Musæum Victorium at Rome is a curious and ancient representation of them in a cement of sulphur and plaster. Their names are engraved beside them, together with certain attributes. Near Constantine and John are two clubs, near Maximian a knotty club, near Malchus and Martinian two axes, near Serapion a burning torch, and near Danesius or Dionysius a great nail, such as those spoken of by Horace (Lib. 1, Od. 3) and St. Paulinus (Nat. 9, or Carm. 24) as having been used for torture.

In this group of figures, the seven are represented as young, without beards, and indeed in ancient martyrologies they are frequently called boys.

It has been inferred from this curious plaster representation, that the seven may have suffered under Decius, A. D. 250, and have been buried in the afore-mentioned cave; whilst the discovery and translation of their relics under Theodosius, in 479, may have given rise to the fable. And this I think probable enough. The story of long sleepers and the number seven connected with it is ancient enough, and dates from heathen mythology.

Like many another ancient myth, it was laid hold of by Christian hands and baptized.

Pliny relates the story of Epimenides the epic poet, who, when tending his sheep one hot day, wearied and oppressed with slumber, retreated into a cave, where he fell asleep. After fifty-seven years he awoke, and found every thing changed. His brother, whom he had left a stripling, was now a hoary man.

Epimenides was reckoned one of the seven sages by those who exclude Periander. He flourished in the time of Solon. After his death, at the age of two hundred and eighty-nine, he was revered as a god, and honored especially by the Athenians.

This story is a version of the older legend of the perpetual sleep of the shepherd Endymion, who was thus preserved in unfading youth and beauty by Jupiter.

According to an Arabic legend, St. George thrice rose from his grave, and was thrice slain.

In Scandinavian mythology we have Siegfrid or Sigurd thus resting, and awaiting his call to come forth and fight. Charlemagne sleeps in the Odenberg in Hess, or in the Untersberg near Salzburg, seated on his throne, with his crown on his head and his sword at his side, waiting till the times of Antichrist are fulfilled, when he will wake and burst forth to avenge the blood of the saints. Ogier the Dane, or Olger Dansk, will in like manner shake off his slumber and come forth from the dream-land of Avallon to avenge the right—O that he had shown himself in the Schleswig-Holstein war!

Well do I remember, as a child, contemplating with wondering awe the great Kyffhäuserberg in Thuringia, for therein, I was told, slept Frederic Barbarossa and his six knights. A shepherd once penetrated into the heart of the mountain by a cave, and discovered therein a hall where sat the emperor at a stone table, and his red beard had grown through the slab. At the tread of the shepherd Frederic awoke from his slumber, and asked, "Do the ravens still fly over the mountains?"

"Sire, they do."

"Then we must sleep another hundred years."

But when his beard has wound itself thrice round the table, then will the emperor awake with his knights, and rush forth to release Germany from its bondage, and exalt it to the first place among the kingdoms of Europe.

In Switzerland slumber three Tells at Rutli, near the Vierwaldstätter-see, waiting for the hour of their country's direst need. A shepherd crept into the cave where they rest. The third Tell rose and asked the time. "Noon," replied the shepherd lad. "The time is not yet come," said Tell, and lay down again.

In Scotland, beneath the Eilden hills, sleeps Thomas of Erceldoune; the murdered French who fell in the Sicilian Vespers at Palermo are also slumbering till the time is come when they may wake to avenge themselves. When Constantinople fell into the hands of the Turks, a priest was celebrating the sacred mysteries at the great silver altar of St. Sophia. The celebrant cried to God to protect the sacred host from profanation. Then the wall opened, and he entered, bearing the Blessed Sacrament. It closed on him, and there he is sleeping with his head bowed before the Body of Our Lord, waiting till the Turk is cast out of Constantinople, and St. Sophia is released from its profanation. God speed the time!

In Bohemia sleep three miners deep in the heart of the Kuttenberg. In North America Rip Van Winkle passed twenty years slumbering in the Katskill mountains. In Portugal it is believed that Sebastian, the chivalrous young monarch who did his best to ruin his country by his rash invasion of Morocco, is sleeping somewhere; but he will wake again to be his country's deliverer in the hour of need. Olaf Tryggvason is waiting a similar occasion in Norway. Even Napoleon Bonaparte is believed among some of the French peasantry to be sleeping on in a like manner.

St. Hippolytus relates that St. John the Divine is slumbering at Ephesus, and Sir John Mandeville relates the circumstances as follows: "From Pathmos men gone unto Ephesim a fair citee and nyghe to the see. And there dyede Seynte Johne, and was buryed behynde the highe Awtiere, in a toumbe. And there is a faire chirche. For Christene mene weren wont to holden that place alweyes. And in the tombe of Seynt John is noughte but manna, that is clept Aungeles mete. For his body was translated into Paradys. And Turkes holden now alle that place and the citee and the Chirche. And all Asie the lesse is yclept Turkye. And ye shalle undrestond, that Seynt Johne bid make his grave there in his Lyf, and leyd himself there-inne all quyk. And therefore somme men seyn, that he dyed noughte, but that he resteth there till the Day of Doom. And forsoothe there is a gret marveule: For men may see there the erthe of the tombe apertly many tymes steren and moven, as there weren quykke thinges undre." The connection of this legend of St. John with Ephesus may have had something to do with turning the seven martyrs of that city into seven sleepers.

The annals of Iceland relate that, in 1403, a Finn of the name of Fethmingr, living in Halogaland, in the North of Norway, happening to enter a cave, fell asleep, and woke not for three whole years, lying with his bow and arrows at his side, untouched by bird or beast.

There certainly are authentic accounts of persons having slept

56

for an extraordinary length of time, but I shall not mention any, as I believe the legend we are considering, not to have been an exaggeration of facts, but a Christianized myth of paganism. The fact of the number seven being so prominent in many of the tales, seems to lead to this conclusion. Barbarossa changes his position every seven years. Charlemagne starts in his chair at similar intervals. Olger Dansk stamps his iron mace on the floor once every seven years. Olaf Redbeard in Sweden uncloses his eyes at precisely the same distances of time.

I believe that the mythological core of this picturesque legend is the repose of the earth through the seven winter months. In the North, Frederic and Charlemagne certainly replace Odin.

The German and Scandinavian still heathen legends represent the heroes as about to issue forth for the defence of Fatherland in the hour of direst need. The converted and Christianized tale brings the martyr youths forth in the hour when a heresy is afflicting the Church, that they may destroy the heresy by their witness to the truth of the Resurrection.

If there is something majestic in the heathen myth, there are singular grace and beauty in the Christian tale, teaching, as it does, such a glorious doctrine; but it is surpassed in delicacy by the modern form which the same myth has assumed—a form which is a real transformation, leaving the doctrine taught the same. It has been made into a romance by Hoffman, and is versified by Trinius. I may perhaps be allowed to translate with some freedom the poem of the latter:—

> In an ancient shaft of Falun
> Year by year a body lay,
> God-preserved, as though a treasure,
> Kept unto the waking day.
>
> Not the turmoil, nor the passions,
> Of the busy world o'erhead,
> Sounds of war, or peace rejoicings,
> Could disturb the placid dead.

Once a youthful miner, whistling,
Hewed the chamber, now his tomb:
Crash! the rocky fragments tumbled,
Closed him in abysmal gloom.

Sixty years passed by, ere miners
Toiling, hundred fathoms deep,
Broke upon the shaft where rested
That poor miner in his sleep.

As the gold-grains lie untarnished
In the dingy soil and sand,
Till they gleam and flicker, stainless,
In the digger's sifting hand;—

As the gem in virgin brilliance
Rests, till ushered into day;—
So uninjured, uncorrupted,
Fresh and fair the body lay.

And the miners bore it upward,
Laid it in the yellow sun;
Up, from out the neighboring houses,
Fast the curious peasants run.

"Who is he?" with eyes they question;
"Who is he?" they ask aloud;
Hush! a wizened hag comes hobbling,
Panting, through the wondering crowd.

O! the cry,—half joy, half sorrow,—
As she flings her at his side:
"John! the sweetheart of my girlhood,
Here am I, am I, thy bride.

"Time on thee has left no traces,
Death from wear has shielded thee;

I am agéd, worn, and wasted,
O! what life has done to me!"

Then his smooth, unfurrowed forehead
Kissed that ancient withered crone;
And the Death which had divided
Now united them in one.

WILLIAM TELL

I SUPPOSE that most people regard William Tell, the hero of Switzerland, as an historical character, and visit the scenes made memorable by his exploits, with corresponding interest, when they undertake the regular Swiss round.

It is one of the painful duties of the antiquarian to dispel many a popular belief, and to probe the groundlessness of many an historical statement. The antiquarian is sometimes disposed to ask with Pilate, "What is truth?" when he finds historical facts crumbling beneath his touch into mythological fables; and he soon learns to doubt and question the most emphatic declarations of, and claims to, reliability.

Sir Walter Raleigh, in his prison, was composing the second volume of his History of the World. Leaning on the sill of his window, he meditated on the duties of the historian to mankind, when suddenly his attention was attracted by a disturbance in the court-yard before his cell. He saw one man strike another whom he supposed by his dress to be an officer; the latter at once drew his sword, and ran the former through the body. The wounded man felled his adversary with a stick, and then sank upon the pavement. At this juncture the guard came up, and carried off the officer insensible, and then the corpse of the man who had been run through.

Next day Raleigh was visited by an intimate friend, to whom he related the circumstances of the quarrel and its issue. To his astonishment, his friend unhesitatingly declared that the prisoner had mistaken the whole series of incidents which had passed before his eyes.

The supposed officer was not an officer at all, but the servant of a foreign ambassador; it was he who had dealt the first blow; he had not drawn his sword, but the other had snatched it from his side, and had run him through the body before any one could interfere; whereupon a stranger from among the crowd knocked the murderer down with his stick, and some of the foreigners belonging to the ambassador's retinue carried off the corpse. The friend of Raleigh added that government had ordered the arrest and immediate trial of the murderer, as the man assassinated was one of the principal servants of the Spanish ambassador.

"Excuse me," said Raleigh, "but I cannot have been deceived as you suppose, for I was eye-witness to the events which took place under my own window, and the man fell there on that spot where you see a paving-stone standing up above the rest."

"My dear Raleigh," replied his friend, "I was sitting on that stone when the fray took place, and I received this slight scratch on my cheek in snatching the sword from the murderer; and upon my word of honor, you have been deceived upon every particular."

Sir Walter, when alone, took up the second volume of his History, which was in MS., and contemplating it, thought—"If I cannot believe my own eyes, how can I be assured of the truth of a tithe of the events which happened ages before I was born?" and he flung the manuscript into the fire.[26]

Now, I think that I can show that the story of William Tell is as fabulous as—what shall I say? any other historical event.

It is almost too well known to need repetition.

In the year 1307, Gessler, Vogt of the Emperor Albert of Hapsburg, set a hat on a pole, as symbol of imperial power, and ordered every one who passed by to do obeisance towards it. A mountaineer of the name of Tell boldly traversed the space before it without saluting the abhorred symbol. By Gessler's command he was at once seized and brought before him. As Tell was known to be an expert archer, he was ordered, by way of punishment, to shoot an apple off the head of his own son. Finding remonstrance vain, he submitted. The apple was placed on the child's head, Tell bent his bow, the arrow sped, and apple and arrow fell together to the ground. But the Vogt noticed that Tell, before shooting, had stuck another arrow into his belt, and he inquired the reason.

---

[26] This anecdote is taken from the Journal de Paris, May, 1787; but whence did the Journal obtain it?

"It was for you," replied the sturdy archer. "Had I shot my child, know that it would not have missed your heart."

This event, observe, took place in the beginning of the fourteenth century. But Saxo Grammaticus, a Danish writer of the twelfth century, tells the story of a hero of his own country, who lived in the tenth century. He relates the incident in horrible style as follows:—

"Nor ought what follows to be enveloped in silence. Toki, who had for some time been in the king's service, had, by his deeds, surpassing those of his comrades, made enemies of his virtues. One day, when he had drunk too much, he boasted to those who sat at table with him, that his skill in archery was such, that with the first shot of an arrow he could hit the smallest apple set on the top of a stick at a considerable distance. His detractors, hearing this, lost no time in conveying what he had said to the king (Harald Bluetooth). But the wickedness of this monarch soon transformed the confidence of the father to the jeopardy of the son, for he ordered the dearest pledge of his life to stand in place of the stick, from whom, if the utterer of the boast did not at his first shot strike down the apple, he should with his head pay the penalty of having made an idle boast. The command of the king urged the soldier to do this, which was so much more than he had undertaken, the detracting artifices of the others having taken advantage of words spoken when he was hardly sober. As soon as the boy was led forth, Toki carefully admonished him to receive the whir of the arrow as calmly as possible, with attentive ears, and without moving his head, lest by a slight motion of the body he should frustrate the experience of his well-tried skill. He also made him stand with his back towards him, lest he should be frightened at the sight of the arrow. Then he drew three arrows from his quiver, and the very first he shot struck the proposed mark. Toki being asked by the king why he had taken so many more arrows out of his quiver, when he was to make but one trial with his bow, 'That I might avenge on thee,' he replied, 'the error of the first, by the points of the others, lest my innocence might happen to be afflicted, and thy injustice go unpunished.'"

The same incident is told of Egil, brother of the mythical Velundr, in the Saga of Thidrik.

In Norwegian history also it appears with variations again and again. It is told of King Olaf the Saint (d. 1030), that, desiring the conversion of a brave heathen named Eindridi, he competed with him in various athletic sports; he swam with him, wrestled, and then shot with him. The king dared Eindridi to strike a writing-tablet from off his son's head with an arrow. Eindridi prepared to attempt the difficult shot. The king bade two men bind the eyes of the child and hold the napkin, so that he might not move when he heard the whistle of the arrow. The king aimed first, and the arrow grazed the lad's head. Eindridi then prepared to shoot; but the mother of the boy interfered, and persuaded the king to abandon this dangerous test of skill. In this version, also, Eindridi is prepared to revenge himself on the king, should the child be injured.

But a closer approximation still to the Tell myth is found in the life of Hemingr, another Norse archer, who was challenged by King Harald, Sigurd's son (d. 1066). The story is thus told:—

"The island was densely overgrown with wood, and the people went into the forest. The king took a spear and set it with its point in the soil, then he laid an arrow on the string and shot up into the air. The arrow turned in the air and came down upon the spear-shaft and stood up in it. Hemingr took another arrow and shot up; his was lost to sight for some while, but it came back and pierced the nick of the king's arrow.... Then the king took a knife and stuck it into an oak; he next drew his bow and planted an arrow in the haft of the knife. Thereupon Hemingr took his arrows. The king stood by him and said, 'They are all inlaid with gold; you are a capital workman.' Hemingr answered, 'They are not my manufacture, but are presents.' He shot, and his arrow cleft the haft, and the point entered the socket of the blade.

"'We must have a keener contest,' said the king, taking an arrow and flushing with anger; then he laid the arrow on the string and drew his bow to the farthest, so that the horns were nearly brought to meet. Away flashed the arrow, and pierced a tender twig. All said that this was a most astonishing feat of dexterity. But

Hemingr shot from a greater distance, and split a hazel nut. All were astonished to see this. Then said the king, 'Take a nut and set it on the head of your brother Bjorn, and aim at it from precisely the same distance. If you miss the mark, then your life goes.'

"Hemingr answered, 'Sire, my life is at your disposal, but I will not adventure that shot.' Then out spake Bjorn—'Shoot, brother, rather than die yourself.' Hemingr said, 'Have you the pluck to stand quite still without shrinking?' 'I will do my best,' said Bjorn. 'Then let the king stand by,' said Hemingr, 'and let him see whether I touch the nut.'

"The king agreed, and bade Oddr Ufeigs' son stand by Bjorn, and see that the shot was fair. Hemingr then went to the spot fixed for him by the king, and signed himself with the cross, saying, 'God be my witness that I had rather die myself than injure my brother Bjorn; let all the blame rest on King Harald.'

"Then Hemingr flung his spear. The spear went straight to the mark, and passed between the nut and the crown of the lad, who was not in the least injured. It flew farther, and stopped not till it fell.

"Then the king came up and asked Oddr what he thought about the shot."

Years after, this risk was revenged upon the hard-hearted monarch. In the battle of Stamfordbridge an arrow from a skilled archer penetrated the windpipe of the king, and it is supposed to have sped, observes the Saga writer, from the bow of Hemingr, then in the service of the English monarch.

The story is related somewhat differently in the Faroe Isles, and is told of Geyti, Aslak's son. The same Harald asks his men if they know who is his match in strength. "Yes," they reply; "there is a peasant's son in the uplands, Geyti, son of Aslak, who is the strongest of men." Forth goes the king, and at last rides up to the house of Aslak. "And where is your youngest son?"

"Alas! alas! he lies under the green sod of Kolrin kirkgarth." "Come, then, and show me his corpse, old man, that I may judge whether he was as stout of limb as men say."

The father puts the king off with the excuse that among so many dead it would be hard to find his boy. So the king rides away over the heath. He meets a stately man returning from the chase, with a bow over his shoulder. "And who art thou, friend?" "Geyti, Aslak's son." The dead man, in short, alive and well. The king tells him he has heard of his prowess, and is come to match his strength with him. So Geyti and the king try a swimming-match.

The king swims well; but Geyti swims better, and in the end gives the monarch such a ducking, that he is borne to his house devoid of sense and motion. Harald swallows his anger, as he had swallowed the water, and bids Geyti shoot a hazel nut from off his brother's head. Aslak's son consents, and invites the king into the forest to witness his dexterity.

> "On the string the shaft he laid,
> And God hath heard his prayer;
> He shot the little nut away,
> Nor hurt the lad a hair."

Next day the king sends for the skilful bowman:—

> "List thee, Geyti, Aslak's son,
> And truly tell to me,
> Wherefore hadst thou arrows twain
> In the wood yestreen with thee?"

The bowman replies,—

> "Therefore had I arrows twain
> Yestreen in the wood with me,
> Had I but hurt my brother dear,
> The other had piercéd thee."

A very similar tale is told also in the celebrated Malleus Maleficarum of a man named Puncher, with this difference, that a coin is placed on the lad's head instead of an apple or a nut. The person who had dared Puncher to the test of skill, inquires the use of the second arrow in his belt, and receives the usual answer, that if the first arrow had missed the coin, the second would have transfixed a certain heart which was destitute of natural feeling.

We have, moreover, our English version of the same story in the venerable ballad of William of Cloudsley.

The Finn ethnologist Castrén obtained the following tale in the Finnish village of Uhtuwa:—

A fight took place between some freebooters and the inhabitants of the village of Alajäwi. The robbers plundered every house, and carried off amongst their captives an old man. As they proceeded with their spoils along the strand of the lake, a lad of twelve years old appeared from among the reeds on the opposite bank, armed with a bow, and amply provided with arrows; he threatened to shoot down the captors unless the old man, his father, were restored to him. The robbers mockingly replied that the aged man would be given to him if he could shoot an apple off his head. The boy accepted the challenge, and on successfully accomplishing it, the surrender of the venerable captive was made.

Farid-Uddin Âttar was a Persian dealer in perfumes, born in the year 1119. He one day was so impressed with the sight of a dervish, that he sold his possessions, and followed righteousness. He composed the poem Mantic Uttaïr, or the language of birds. Observe, the Persian Âttar lived at the same time as the Danish Saxo, and long before the birth of Tell. Curiously enough, we find a trace of the Tell myth in the pages of his poem. According to him, however, the king shoots the apple from the head of a beloved page, and the lad dies from sheer fright, though the arrow does not even graze his skin.

The coincidence of finding so many versions of the same story scattered through countries as remote as Persia and Iceland, Switzerland and Denmark, proves, I think, that it can in no way be regarded as history, but is rather one of the numerous household myths common to the whole stock of Aryan nations. Probably, some one more acquainted with Sanskrit literature than myself, and with better access to its unpublished stores of fable and legend, will some day light on an early Indian tale corresponding to that so prevalent among other branches of the same family. The coincidence of the Tell myth being discovered among the Finns is attributable to Russian or Swedish influence. I do not regard it as a primeval Turanian, but as an Aryan story, which, like an erratic block, is found deposited on foreign soil far from the mountain whence it was torn.

German mythologists, I suppose, consider the myth to represent the manifestation of some natural phenomena, and the individuals of the story to be impersonifications of natural forces. Most primeval stories were thus constructed, and their origin is traceable enough. In Thorn-rose, for instance, who can fail to see the earth goddess represented by the sleeping beauty in her long winter slumber, only returning to life when kissed by the golden-haired sun-god Phœbus or Baldur? But the Tell myth has not its signification thus painted on the surface; and those who suppose Gessler or Harald to be the power of evil and darkness,—the bold archer to be the storm-cloud with his arrow of lightning and his iris bow, bent against the sun, which is resting like a coin or a golden apple on the edge of the horizon, are over-straining their theories, and exacting too much from our credulity.

In these pages and elsewhere I have shown how some of the ancient myths related by the whole Aryan family of nations are reducible to allegorical explanations of certain well-known natural phenomena; but I must protest against the manner in which our German friends fasten rapaciously upon every atom of history, sacred and profane, and demonstrate all heroes to represent the sun; all villains to be the demons of night or winter; all sticks and spears and arrows to be the lightning; all cows and sheep and dragons and swans to be clouds.

In a work on the superstition of Werewolves, I have entered into this subject with some fulness, and am quite prepared to admit the premises upon which mythologists construct their theories; at the same time I am not disposed to run to the extravagant lengths reached by some of the most enthusiastic German scholars. A wholesome warning to these gentlemen was given some years ago by an ingenious French ecclesiastic, who wrote the following argument to prove that Napoleon Bonaparte was a mythological character. Archbishop Whately's "Historic Doubts" was grounded on a totally different line of argument; I subjoin the other, as a curiosity and as a caution.

Napoleon is, says the writer, an impersonification of the sun.

1. Between the name Napoleon and Apollo, or Apoleon, the god of the sun, there is but a trifling difference; indeed, the seeming difference is lessened, if we take the spelling of his name from the column of the Place Vendôme, where it stands Néapoleó. But this syllable Ne prefixed to the name of the sun-god is of importance; like the rest of the name it is of Greek origin, and is νη or ναι, a particle of affirmation, as though indicating Napoleon as the very true Apollo, or sun.

His other name, Bonaparte, makes this apparent connection between the French hero and the luminary of the firmament conclusively certain. The day has its two parts, the good and luminous portion, and that which is bad and dark. To the sun belongs the good part, to the moon and stars belongs the bad portion. It is therefore natural that Apollo or Né-Apoleón should receive the surname of Bonaparte.

2. Apollo was born in Delos, a Mediterranean island; Napoleon in Corsica, an island in the same sea. According to Pausanias, Apollo was an Egyptian deity; and in the mythological history of the fabulous Napoleon we find the hero in Egypt, regarded by the inhabitants with veneration, and receiving their homage.

3. The mother of Napoleon was said to be Letitia, which signifies joy, and is an impersonification of the dawn of light dispensing joy and gladness to all creation. Letitia is no other than the break of day, which in a manner brings the sun into the world, and "with rosy fingers opes the gates of Day." It is significant that the Greek name for the mother of Apollo was Leto. From this the Romans made the name Latona, which they gave to his mother. But Læto is the unused form of the verb lætor, and signified to inspire joy; it is from this unused form that the substantive Letitia is derived. The identity, then, of the mother of Napoleon with the Greek Leto and the Latin Latona, is established conclusively.

4. According to the popular story, this son of Letitia had three sisters; and was it not the same with the Greek deity, who had the three Graces?

5. The modern Gallic Apollo had four brothers. It is impossible not to discern here the anthropomorphosis of the four seasons. But, it will be objected, the seasons should be females. Here the French language interposes; for in French the seasons are masculine, with the exception of autumn, upon the gender of which grammarians are undecided, whilst Autumnus in Latin is not more feminine than the other seasons. This difficulty is therefore trifling, and what follows removes all shadow of doubt.

Of the four brothers of Napoleon, three are said to have been kings, and these of course are, Spring reigning over the flowers, Summer reigning over the harvest, Autumn holding sway over the fruits. And as these three seasons owe all to the powerful influence of the Sun, we are told in the popular myth that the three brothers of Napoleon drew their authority from him, and received from him their kingdoms. But if it be added that, of the four brothers of Napoleon, one was not a king, that was because he is the impersonification of Winter, which has no reign over anything. If, however, it be asserted, in contradiction, that the winter has an empire, he will be given the principality over snows and frosts, which, in the dreary season of the year, whiten the face of the earth. Well, the fourth brother of Napoleon is thus invested by popular tradition, commonly called history, with a vain principality accorded to him in the decline of the power of Napoleon. The principality was that of Canino, a name derived from cani, or the whitened hairs of a frozen old age,—true emblem of winter. To the eyes of poets, the forests covering the hills are their hair, and when winter frosts them, they represent the snowy locks of a decrepit nature in the old age of the year:—

"Cum gelidus crescit canis in montibus humor."

Consequently the Prince of Canino is an impersonification of winter;—winter whose reign begins when the kingdoms of the three fine seasons are passed from them, and when the sun is driven from his power by the children of the North, as the poets call the boreal winds. This is the origin of the fabulous invasion of France by the allied armies of the North. The story relates that these invaders—the northern gales—banished the many-colored flag, and replaced it by a white standard. This too is a graceful, but, at the same time, purely fabulous account of the Northern winds driving all the brilliant colors from the face of the soil, to replace them by the snowy sheet.

6. Napoleon is said to have had two wives. It is well known that the classic fable gave two also to Apollo. These two were the moon and the earth. Plutarch asserts that the Greeks gave the moon to Apollo for wife, whilst the Egyptians attributed to him the earth. By the moon he had no posterity, but by the other he had one son only, the little Horus. This is an Egyptian allegory, representing the fruits of agriculture produced by the earth fertilized by the Sun. The pretended son of the fabulous Napoleon is said to have been born on the 20th of March, the season of the spring equinox, when agriculture is assuming its greatest period of activity.

7. Napoleon is said to have released France from the devastating scourge which terrorized over the country, the hydra of the revolution, as it was popularly called. Who cannot see in this a Gallic version of the Greek legend of Apollo releasing Hellas from the terrible Python? The very name revolution, derived from the Latin verb revolvo, is indicative of the coils of a serpent like the Python.

8. The famous hero of the 19th century had, it is asserted, twelve Marshals at the head of his armies, and four who were stationary and inactive. The twelve first, as may be seen at once, are the signs of the zodiac, marching under the orders of the sun Napoleon, and each commanding a division of the innumerable host of stars, which are parted into twelve portions, corresponding to the twelve signs. As for the four stationary officers, immovable in the midst of general motion, they are the cardinal points.

9. It is currently reported that the chief of these brilliant armies, after having gloriously traversed the Southern kingdoms, penetrated North, and was there unable to maintain his sway. This too represents the course of the Sun, which assumes its greatest power in the South, but after the spring equinox seeks to reach the North; and after a three months' march towards the boreal regions, is driven back upon his traces following the sign of Cancer, a sign

given to represent the retrogression of the sun in that portion of the sphere. It is on this that the story of the march of Napoleon towards Moscow, and his humbling retreat, is founded.

10. Finally, the sun rises in the East and sets in the Western sea. The poets picture him rising out of the waters in the East, and setting in the ocean after his twelve hours' reign in the sky. Such is the history of Napoleon, coming from his Mediterranean isle, holding the reins of government for twelve years, and finally disappearing in the mysterious regions of the great Atlantic.

To those who see in Samson, the image of the sun, the correlative of the classic Hercules, this clever skit of the accomplished French Abbé may prove of value as a caution.

THE DOG GELLERT

HAVING demolished William Tell, I proceed to the destruction of another article of popular belief.

Who that has visited Snowdon has not seen the grave of Llewellyn's faithful hound Gellert, and been told by the guide the touching story of the death of the noble animal? How can we doubt the facts, seeing that the place, Beth-Gellert, is named after the dog, and that the grave is still visible? But unfortunately for the truth of the legend, its pedigree can be traced with the utmost precision.

The story is as follows:—

The Welsh Prince Llewellyn had a noble deerhound, Gellert, whom he trusted to watch the cradle of his baby son whilst he himself was absent.

One day, on his return, to his intense horror, he beheld the cradle empty and upset, the clothes dabbled with blood, and Gellert's mouth dripping with gore. Concluding hastily that the hound had proved unfaithful, had fallen on the child and devoured it,—in a paroxysm of rage the prince drew his sword and slew the dog. Next instant the cry of the babe from behind the cradle showed him that the child was uninjured; and, on looking farther, Llewellyn discovered the body of a huge wolf, which had entered the house to seize and devour the child, but which had been kept off and killed by the brave dog Gellert.

In his self-reproach and grief, the prince erected a stately monument to Gellert, and called the place where he was buried after the poor hound's name.

Now, I find in Russia precisely the same story told, with just the same appearance of truth, of a Czar Piras. In Germany it appears with considerable variations. A man determines on slaying his old dog Sultan, and consults with his wife how this is to be effected. Sultan overhears the conversation, and complains bitterly to the wolf, who suggests an ingenious plan by which the master may be induced to spare his dog. Next day, when the man is going to his work, the wolf undertakes to carry off the child from its cradle. Sultan is to attack him and rescue the infant. The plan succeeds admirably, and the dog spends his remaining years in comfort. (Grimm, K. M. 48.)

But there is a story in closer conformity to that of Gellert among the French collections of fabliaux made by Le Grand d'Aussy and Edéléstand du Méril. It became popular through the "Gesta Romanorum," a collection of tales made by the monks for harmless reading, in the fourteenth century.

In the "Gesta" the tale is told as follows:—

"Folliculus, a knight, was fond of hunting and tournaments. He had an only son, for whom three nurses were provided. Next to this child, he loved his falcon and his greyhound. It happened one day that he was called to a tournament, whither his wife and domestics went also, leaving the child in the cradle, the greyhound lying by him, and the falcon on his perch. A serpent that inhabited a hole near the castle, taking advantage of the profound silence that reigned, crept from his habitation, and advanced towards the cradle to devour the child. The falcon, perceiving the danger, fluttered with his wings till he awoke the dog, who instantly attacked the invader, and after a fierce conflict, in which he was sorely wounded, killed him. He then lay down on the ground to lick and heal his wounds. When the nurses returned, they found the cradle overturned, the child thrown out, and the ground covered with blood, as was also the dog, who they immediately concluded had killed the child.

"Terrified at the idea of meeting the anger of the parents, they determined to escape; but in their flight fell in with their mistress, to whom they were compelled to relate the supposed murder of the child by the greyhound. The knight soon arrived to hear the sad story, and, maddened with fury, rushed forward to the spot. The poor wounded and faithful animal made an effort to rise and welcome his master with his accustomed fondness; but the enraged knight received him on the point of his sword, and he fell lifeless to the ground. On examination of the cradle, the infant was found alive and unhurt, with the dead serpent lying by him. The knight now perceived what had happened, lamented bitterly over his faithful dog, and blamed himself for having too hastily depended on the words of his wife. Abandoning the profession of arms, he broke his lance in pieces, and vowed a pilgrimage to the Holy Land, where he spent the rest of his days in peace."

The monkish hit at the wife is amusing, and might have been supposed to have originated with those determined misogynists, as the gallant Welshmen lay all the blame on the man. But the good compilers of the "Gesta" wrote little of their own, except moral applications of the tales they relate, and the story of Folliculus and his dog, like many others in their collection, is drawn from a foreign source.

It occurs in the Seven Wise Masters, and in the "Calumnia Novercalis" as well, so that it must have been popular throughout mediæval Europe. Now, the tales of the Seven Wise Masters are translations from a Hebrew work, the Kalilah and Dimnah of Rabbi Joel, composed about A. D. 1250, or from Simeon Seth's Greek Kylile and Dimne, written in 1080. These Greek and Hebrew works were derived from kindred sources. That of Rabbi Joel was a translation from an Arabic version made by Nasr-Allah in the twelfth century, whilst Simeon Seth's was a translation of the Persian Kalilah and Dimnah. But the Persian Kalilah and Dimnah was not either an original work; it was in turn a translation from the Sanskrit Pantschatantra, made about A. D. 540.

In this ancient Indian book the story runs as follows:—

A Brahmin named Devasaman had a wife, who gave birth to a son, and also to an ichneumon. She loved both her children dearly, giving them alike the breast, and anointing them alike with salves. But she feared the ichneumon might not love his brother.

One day, having laid her boy in bed, she took up the water jar, and said to her husband, "Hear me, master! I am going to the tank to fetch water. Whilst I am absent, watch the boy, lest he gets injured by the ichneumon." After she had left the house, the Brahmin went forth begging, leaving the house empty. In crept a black snake, and attempted to bite the child; but the ichneumon rushed at it, and tore it in pieces. Then, proud of its achievement, it sallied forth, all bloody, to meet its mother. She, seeing the creature stained with blood, concluded, with feminine precipitance, that it had fallen on the baby and killed it, and she flung her water jar at it and slew it. Only on her return home did she ascertain her mistake.

The same story is also told in the Hitopadesa (iv. 13), but the animal is an otter, not an ichneumon. In the Arabic version a weasel takes the place of the ichneumon.

The Buddhist missionaries carried the story into Mongolia, and in the Mongolian Uligerun, which is a translation of the Tibetian Dsanghen, the story reappears with the pole-cat as the brave and suffering defender of the child.

Stanislaus Julien, the great Chinese scholar, has discovered the same tale in the Chinese work entitled "The Forest of Pearls from the Garden of the Law." This work dates from 668; and in it the creature is an ichneumon.

In the Persian Sindibad-nâmeh is the same tale, but the faithful animal is a cat. In Sandabar and Syntipas it has become a dog. Through the influence of Sandabar on the Hebrew translation of the Kalilah and Dimnah, the ichneumon is also replaced by a dog.

Such is the history of the Gellert legend; it is an introduction into Europe from India, every step of its transmission being clearly demonstrable. From the Gesta Romanorum it passed into a popular tale throughout Europe, and in different countries it was, like the Tell myth, localized and individualized. Many a Welsh story, such as those contained in the Mabinogion, are as easily traced to an Eastern origin.

But every story has its root. The root of the Gellert tale is this: A man forms an alliance of friendship with a beast or bird. The dumb animal renders him a signal service. He misunderstands the act, and kills his preserver.

We have tracked this myth under the Gellert form from India to Wales; but under another form it is the property of the whole Aryan family, and forms a portion of the traditional lore of all nations sprung from that stock.

Thence arose the classic fable of the peasant, who, as he slept, was bitten by a fly. He awoke, and in a rage killed the insect. When too late, he observed that the little creature had aroused him that he might avoid a snake which lay coiled up near his pillow.

In the Anvar-i-Suhaili is the following kindred tale. A king had a falcon. One day, whilst hunting, he filled a goblet with water dropping from a rock. As he put the vessel to his lips, his falcon dashed upon it, and upset it with its wings. The king, in a fury, slew the bird, and then discovered that the water dripped from the jaws of a serpent of the most poisonous description.

This story, with some variations, occurs in Æsop, Ælian, and Apthonius. In the Greek fable, a peasant liberates an eagle from the clutches of a dragon. The dragon spirts poison into the water which the peasant is about to drink, without observing what the monster had done. The grateful eagle upsets the goblet with his wings.

The story appears in Egypt under a whimsical form. A Wali once smashed a pot full of herbs which a cook had prepared. The exasperated cook thrashed the well-intentioned but unfortunate Wali within an inch of his life, and when he returned, exhausted with his efforts at belaboring the man, to examine the broken pot, he discovered amongst the herbs a poisonous snake.

How many brothers, sisters, uncles, aunts, and cousins of all degrees a little story has! And how few of the tales we listen to can lay any claim to originality! There is scarcely a story which I hear which I cannot connect with some family of myths, and whose pedigree I cannot ascertain with more or less precision. Shakespeare drew the plots of his plays from Boccaccio or Straparola; but these Italians did not invent the tales they lent to the English dramatist. King Lear does not originate with Geofry of Monmouth, but comes from early Indian stores of fable, whence also are derived the Merchant of Venice and the pound of flesh, ay, and the very incident of the three caskets.

But who would credit it, were it not proved by conclusive facts, that Johnny Sands is the inheritance of the whole Aryan family of nations, and that Peeping Tom of Coventry peeped in India and on the Tartar steppes ages before Lady Godiva was born?

If you listen to Traviata at the opera, you have set before you a tale which has lasted for centuries, and which was perhaps born in India.

If you read in classic fable of Orpheus charming woods and meadows, beasts and birds, with his magic lyre, you remember to have seen the same fable related in the Kalewala of the Finnish Wainomainen, and in the Kaleopoeg of the Esthonian Kalewa.

If you take up English history, and read of William the Conqueror slipping as he landed on British soil, and kissing the earth, saying he had come to greet and claim his own, you remember that the same story is told of Napoleon in Egypt, of King Olaf Harold's son in Norway, and in classic history of Junius Brutus on his return from the oracle.

A little while ago I cut out of a Sussex newspaper a story purporting to be the relation of a fact which had taken place at a fixed date in Lewes. This was the story. A tyrannical husband locked the door against his wife, who was out having tea with a neighbor, gossiping and scandal-mongering; when she applied for admittance, he pretended not to know her. She threatened to jump into the well unless he opened the door.

The man, not supposing that she would carry her threat into execution, declined, alleging that he was in bed, and the night was chilly; besides which he entirely disclaimed all acquaintance with the lady who claimed admittance.

The wife then flung a log into a well, and secreted herself behind the door. The man, hearing the splash, fancied that his good lady was really in the deeps, and forth he darted in his nocturnal costume, which was of the lightest, to ascertain whether his deliverance was complete. At once the lady darted into the house, locked the door, and, on the husband pleading for admittance, she declared most solemnly from the window that she did not know him.

Now, this story, I can positively assert, unless the events of this world move in a circle, did not happen in Lewes, or any other Sussex town.

It was told in the Gesta Romanorum six hundred years ago, and it was told, may be, as many hundred years before in India, for it is still to be found in Sanskrit collections of tales.

TAILED MEN

I WELL remember having it impressed upon me by a Devonshire nurse, as a little child, that all Cornishmen were born with tails; and it was long before I could overcome the prejudice thus early implanted in my breast against my Cornubian neighbors. I looked upon those who dwelt across the Tamar as "uncanny," as being scarcely to be classed with Christian people, and certainly not to be freely associated with by tailless Devonians. I think my eyes were first opened to the fact that I had been deceived by a worthy bookseller of L——, with whom I had contracted a warm friendship, he having at sundry times contributed pictures to my scrapbook. I remember one day resolving to broach the delicate subject with my tailed friend, whom I liked, notwithstanding his caudal appendage.

"Mr. X——, is it true that you are a Cornishman?"

"Yes, my little man; born and bred in the West country."

"I like you very much; but—have you really got a tail?"

When the bookseller had recovered from the astonishment which I had produced by my question, he stoutly repudiated the charge.

"But you are a Cornishman?"

"To be sure I am."

"And all Cornishmen have tails."

I believe I satisfied my own mind that the good man had sat his off, and my nurse assured me that such was the case with those of sedentary habits.

It is curious that Devonshire superstition should attribute the tail to Cornishmen, for it was asserted of certain men of Kent in olden times, and was referred to Divine vengeance upon them for having insulted St. Thomas à Becket, if we may believe Polydore Vergil. "There were some," he says, "to whom it seemed that the king's secret wish was, that Thomas should be got rid of. He, indeed, as one accounted to be an enemy of the king's person, was already regarded with so little respect, nay, was treated with so much contempt, that when he came to Strood, which village is situated on the Medway, the river that washes Rochester, the inhabitants of the place, being eager to show some mark of contumely to the prelate in his disgrace, did not scruple to cut off the tail of the horse on which he was riding; but by this profane and inhospitable act they covered themselves with eternal reproach; for it so happened after this, by the will of God, that all the offspring born from the men who had done this thing, were born with tails, like brute animals. But this mark of infamy, which formerly was everywhere notorious, has disappeared with the extinction of the race whose fathers perpetrated this deed."

John Bale, the zealous reformer, and Bishop of Ossory in Edward VI.'s time, refers to this story, and also mentions a variation of the scene and cause of this ignoble punishment. He writes, quoting his authorities, "John Capgrave and Alexander of Esseby sayth, that for castynge of fyshe tayles at thys Augustyne, Dorsettshyre men had tayles ever after. But Polydorus applieth it unto Kentish men at Stroud, by Rochester, for cuttinge off Thomas Becket's horse's tail. Thus hath England in all other land a perpetual infamy of tayles by theye wrytten legendes of lyes, yet can they not well tell where to bestowe them truely." Bale, a fierce and unsparing reformer, and one who stinted not hard words, applying to the inventors of these legends an epithet more strong than elegant, says, "In the legends of their sanctified sorcerers they have diffamed the English posterity with tails, as has been showed afore. That an Englyshman now cannot travayle in another land by way of marchandyse or any other honest occupyinge, but it is most contumeliously thrown in his tethe that all Englyshmen have tails. That uncomely note and report have the nation gotten, without recover, by these laisy and idle lubbers, the monkes and the priestes, which could find no matters to advance their canonized gains by, or their saintes, as they call them, but manifest lies and knaveries."[27]

---

[27] "Actes of English Votaries."

Andrew Marvel also makes mention of this strange judgment in his Loyal Scot:—

> "But who considers right will find, indeed,
> 'Tis Holy Island parts us, not the Tweed.
> Nothing but clergy could us two seclude,
> No Scotch was ever like a bishop's feud.
> All Litanys in this have wanted faith,
> There's no—Deliver us from a Bishop's wrath.
> Never shall Calvin pardoned be for sales,
> Never, for Burnet's sake, the Lauderdales;
> For Becket's sake, Kent always shall have tails."

It may be remembered that Lord Monboddo, a Scotch judge of last century, and a philosopher of some repute, though of great eccentricity, stoutly maintained the theory that man ought to have a tail, that the tail is a desideratum, and that the abrupt termination of the spine without caudal elongation is a sad blemish in the origination of man. The tail, the point in which man is inferior to the brute, what a delicate index of the mind it is! how it expresses the passions of love and hate! how nicely it gives token of the feelings of joy or fear which animate the soul! But Lord Monboddo did not consider that what the tail is to the brute, that the eye is to man; the lack of one member is supplied by the other. I can tell a proud man by his eye just as truly as if he stalked past one with erect tail; and anger is as plainly depicted in the human eye as in the bottle-brush tail of a cat. I know a sneak by his cowering glance, though he has not a tail between his legs; and pleasure is evident in the laughing eye, without there being any necessity for a wagging brush to express it.

Dr. Johnson paid a visit to the judge, and knocked on the head his theory that men ought to have tails, and actually were born with them occasionally; for said he, "Of a standing fact, sir, there ought to be no controversy; if there are men with tails, catch a homo caudatus." And, "It is a pity to see Lord Monboddo publish such notions as he has done—a man of sense, and of so much elegant learning. There would be little in a fool doing it; we should only laugh; but, when a wise man does it, we are sorry. Other people have strange notions, but they conceal them. If they have tails they hide them; but Monboddo is as jealous of his tail as a squirrel." And yet Johnson seems to have been tickled with the idea, and to have been amused with the notion of an appendage like a tail being regarded as the complement of human perfection. It may be remembered how Johnson made the acquaintance of the young Laird of Col, during his Highland tour, and how pleased he was with him. "Col," says he, "is a noble animal. He is as complete an islander as the mind can figure. He is a farmer, a sailor, a hunter, a fisher: he will run you down a dog; if any man has a tail, it is Col." And notwithstanding all his aversion to puns, the great Doctor was fain to yield to human weakness on one occasion, under the influence of the mirth which Monboddo's name seems to have excited. Johnson writes to Mrs. Thrale of a party he had met one night, which he thus enumerates: "There were Smelt, and the Bishop of St. Asaph, who comes to every place; and Sir Joshua, and Lord Monboddo, and ladies out of tale."

There is a Polish story of a witch who made a girdle of human skin and laid it across the threshold of a door where a marriage-feast was being held. On the bridal pair stepping across the girdle they were transformed into wolves. Three years after the witch sought them out, and cast over them dresses of fur with the hair turned outward, whereupon they recovered their human forms, but, unfortunately, the dress cast over the bridegroom was too scanty, and did not extend over his tail, so that, when he was restored to his former condition, he retained his lupine caudal appendage, and this became hereditary in his family; so that all Poles with tails are lineal descendants of the ancestor to whom this little misfortune happened. John Struys, a Dutch traveller, who visited the Isle of Formosa in 1677, gives a curious story, which is worth transcribing.

"Before I visited this island," he writes, "I had often heard tell that there were men who had long tails, like brute beasts; but I had never been able to believe it, and I regarded it as a thing so alien to our nature, that I should now have difficulty in accepting it, if my own senses had not removed from me every pretence for doubting the fact, by the following strange adventure: The inhabitants of Formosa, being used to see us, were in the habit of receiving us on terms which left nothing to apprehend on either side; so that, although mere foreigners, we always believed ourselves in safety, and had grown familiar enough to ramble at large without an escort, when grave experience taught us that, in so doing, we were hazarding too much. As some of our party were one day taking a stroll, one of them had occasion to withdraw about a stone's throw from the rest, who, being at the moment engaged in an eager conversation, proceeded without heeding the disappearance of their companion. After a while, however, his absence was observed, and the party paused, thinking he would rejoin them. They waited some time; but at last, tired of the delay, they returned in the direction of the spot where they remembered to have seen him last. Arriving there, they were horrified to find his mangled body lying on the ground, though the nature of the lacerations showed that he had not had to suffer long ere death released him. Whilst some remained to watch the dead body, others went off in search of the murderer; and these had not gone far, when they came upon a man of peculiar appearance, who, finding himself enclosed by the exploring party, so as to make escape from them impossible, began to foam with rage, and by cries and wild gesticulations to intimate that he would make any one repent the attempt who should venture to meddle with him. The fierceness of his desperation for a time kept our people at bay; but as his fury gradually subsided, they gathered more closely round him, and at length seized him. He then soon made them understand that it was he who had killed their comrade, but they could not learn from him any cause for this conduct. As the crime was so atrocious, and, if allowed to pass with impunity, might entail even more serious consequences, it was determined to burn the man. He was tied up to a stake, where he was kept for some hours before the time of execution arrived. It was then that I beheld what I had never thought to see. He had a tail more than a foot long, covered with red hair, and very like that of a cow. When he saw the surprise that this discovery created among the European spectators, he informed us that his tail was the effect of climate, for that all the inhabitants of the southern side of the island, where they then were, were provided with like appendages."[28]

After Struys, Hornemann reported that, between the Gulf of Benin and Abyssinia, were tailed anthropophagi, named by the natives Niam-niams; and in 1849, M. Descouret, on his return from Mecca, affirmed that such was a common report, and added that they had long arms, low and narrow foreheads, long and erect ears, and slim legs.

Mr. Harrison, in his "Highlands of Ethiopia," alludes to the common belief among the Abyssinians, in a pygmy race of this nature.

MM. Arnault and Vayssière, travellers in the same country, in 1850, brought the subject before the Academy of Sciences.

In 1851, M. de Castelnau gave additional details relative to an expedition against these tailed men. "The Niam-niams," he says, "were sleeping in the sun: the Haoussas approached, and, falling on them, massacred them to the last man. They had all of them tails forty centimetres long, and from two to three in diameter. This organ is smooth. Among the corpses were those of several women, who were deformed in the same manner. In all other particulars, the men were precisely like all other negroes. They are of a deep black, their teeth are polished, their bodies not tattooed. They are armed with clubs and javelins; in war they utter piercing cries. They cultivate rice, maize, and other grain. They are fine looking men, and their hair is not frizzled."

M. d'Abbadie, another Abyssinian traveller, writing in 1852, gives the following account from the lips of an Abyssinian priest: "At the distance of fifteen days' journey south of Herrar is a place where all the men have tails, the length of a palm, covered with hair, and situated at the extremity of the spine. The females of that country are very beautiful and are tailless. I have seen some fifteen of these people at Besberah, and I am positive that the tail is natural."

It will be observed that there is a discrepancy between the accounts of M. de Castelnau and M. d'Abbadie. The former accords

---

[28] "Voyages de Jean Struys," An. 1650.

tails to the ladies, whilst the latter denies it. According to the former, the tail is smooth; according to the latter, it is covered with hair.

Dr. Wolf has improved on this in his "Travels and Adventures," vol. ii. 1861. "There are men and women in Abyssinia with tails like dogs and horses." Wolf heard also from a great many Abyssinians and Armenians (and Wolf is convinced of the truth of it), that "there are near Narea, in Abyssinia, people—men and women—with large tails, with which they are able to knock down a horse; and there are also such people near China." And in a note, "In the College of Surgeons at Dublin may still be seen a human skeleton, with a tail seven inches long! There are many known instances of this elongation of the caudal vertebra, as in the Poonangs in Borneo."

But the most interesting and circumstantial account of the Niam-niams is that given by Dr. Hubsch, physician to the hospitals of Constantinople. "It was in 1852," says he, "that I saw for the first time a tailed negress. I was struck with this phenomenon, and I questioned her master, a slave dealer. I learned from him that there exists a tribe called Niam-niam, occupying the interior of Africa. All the members of this tribe bear the caudal appendage, and, as Oriental imagination is given to exaggeration, I was assured that the tails sometimes attained the length of two feet. That which I observed was smooth and hairless. It was about two inches long, and terminated in a point. This woman was as black as ebony, her hair was frizzled, her teeth white, large, and planted in sockets which inclined considerably outward; her four canine teeth were filed, her eyes bloodshot. She ate meat raw, her clothes fidgeted her, her intellect was on a par with that of others of her condition.

"Her master had been unable, during six months, to sell her, notwithstanding the low figure at which he would have disposed of her; the abhorrence with which she was regarded was not attributed to her tail, but to the partiality, which she was unable to conceal, for human flesh. Her tribe fed on the flesh of the prisoners taken from the neighboring tribes, with whom they were constantly at war.

"As soon as one of the tribe dies, his relations, instead of burying him, cut him up and regale themselves upon his remains; consequently there are no cemeteries in this land. They do not all of them lead a wandering life, but many of them construct hovels of the branches of trees. They make for themselves weapons of war and of agriculture; they cultivate maize and wheat, and keep cattle. The Niam-niams have a language of their own, of an entirely primitive character, though containing an infusion of Arabic words.

"They live in a state of complete nudity, and seek only to satisfy their brute appetites. There is among them an utter disregard for morality, incest and adultery being common. The strongest among them becomes the chief of the tribe; and it is he who apportions the shares of the booty obtained in war. It is hard to say whether they have any religion; but in all probability they have none, as they readily adopt any one which they are taught.

"It is difficult to tame them altogether; their instinct impelling them constantly to seek for human flesh; and instances are related of slaves who have massacred and eaten the children confided to their charge.

"I have seen a man of the same race, who had a tail an inch and a half long, covered with a few hairs. He appeared to be thirty-five years old; he was robust, well built, of an ebon blackness, and had the same peculiar formation of jaw noticed above; that is to say, the tooth sockets were inclined outwards. Their four canine teeth are filed down, to diminish their power of mastication.

"I know also, at Constantinople, the son of a physician, aged two years, who was born with a tail an inch long; he belonged to the white Caucasian race. One of his grandfathers possessed the same appendage. This phenomenon is regarded generally in the East as a sign of great brute force."

About ten years ago, a newspaper paragraph recorded the birth of a boy at Newcastle-on-Tyne, provided with a tail about an inch and a quarter long. It was asserted that the child when sucking wagged this stump as token of pleasure.

Yet, notwithstanding all this testimony in favor of tailed men and women, it is simply a matter of impossibility for a human being to have a tail, for the spinal vertebræ in man do not admit of elongation, as in many animals; for the spine terminates in the os sacrum, a large and expanded bone of peculiar character, entirely precluding all possibility of production to the spine as in caudate animals.

ANTICHRIST AND POPE JOAN

FROM the earliest ages of the Church, the advent of the Man of Sin has been looked forward to with terror, and the passages of Scripture relating to him have been studied with solemn awe, lest that day of wrath should come upon the Church unawares. As events in the world's history took place which seemed to be indications of the approach of Antichrist, a great horror fell upon men's minds, and their imaginations conjured up myths which flew from mouth to mouth, and which were implicitly believed.

Before speaking of these strange tales which produced such an effect on the minds of men in the middle ages, it will be well briefly to examine the opinions of divines of the early ages on the passages of Scripture connected with the coming of the last great persecutor of the Church. Antichrist was believed by most ancient writers to be destined to arise out of the tribe of Dan, a belief founded on the prediction of Jacob, "Dan shall be a serpent by the way, an adder in the path" (conf. Jeremiah viii. 16), and on the exclamation of the dying patriarch, when looking on his son Dan, "I have waited for Thy Salvation, O Lord," as though the long-suffering of God had borne long with that tribe, but in vain, and it was to be extinguished without hope. This, indeed, is implied in the sealing of the servants of God in their foreheads (Revelation vii.), when twelve thousand out of every tribe, except Dan, were seen by St. John to receive the seal of adoption, whilst of the tribe of Dan not one was sealed, as though it, to a man, had apostatized.

Opinions as to the nature of Antichrist were divided. Some held that he was to be a devil in phantom body, and of this number was Hippolytus. Others, again, believed that he would be an incarnate demon, true man and true devil; in fearful and diabolical parody of the Incarnation of our Lord. A third view was, that he would be merely a desperately wicked man, acting upon diabolical inspirations, just as the saints act upon divine inspirations. St. John Damascene expressly asserts that he will not be an incarnate demon, but a devilish man; for he says, "Not as Christ assumed humanity, so will the devil become human, but the Man will receive all the inspiration of Satan, and will suffer the devil to take up his abode within him." In this manner Antichrist could have many forerunners; and so St. Jerome and St. Augustine saw an Antichrist in Nero, not the Antichrist, but one of those of whom the Apostle speaks—"Even now are there many Antichrists." Thus also every enemy of the faith, such as Diocletian, Julian, and Mahomet, has been regarded as a precursor of the Arch-persecutor, who was expected to sum up in himself the cruelty of a Nero or Diocletian, the show of virtue of a Julian, and the spiritual pride of a Mahomet.

From infancy the evil one is to take possession of Antichrist, and to train him for his office, instilling into him cunning, cruelty, and pride. His doctrine will be—not downright infidelity, but a "show of godliness," whilst "denying the power thereof;" i. e., the miraculous origin and divine authority of Christianity. He will sow doubts of our Lord's manifestation "in the flesh," he will allow Christ to be an excellent Man, capable of teaching the most exalted truths, and inculcating the purest morality, yet Himself fallible and carried away by fanaticism.

In the end, however, Antichrist will "exalt himself to sit as God in the temple of God," and become "the abomination of desolation standing in the holy place." At the same time there is to be an awful alliance struck between himself, the impersonification of the world-power and the Church of God; some high pontiff of which, or the episcopacy in general, will enter into league with the unbelieving state to oppress the very elect. It is a strange instance of religionary virulence which makes some detect the Pope of Rome in the Man of Sin, the Harlot, the Beast, and the Priest going before it. The Man of Sin and the Beast are unmistakably identical, and refer to an Antichristian world-power; whilst the Harlot and the Priest are symbols of an apostasy in the Church. There is nothing Roman in this, but something very much the opposite.

How the Abomination of Desolation can be considered as set up in a Church where every sanctuary is adorned with all that can draw the heart to the Crucified, and raise the thoughts to the imposing ritual of Heaven, is a puzzle to me. To the man uninitiated in the law that Revelation is to be interpreted by contraries, it would seem more like the Abomination of Desolation in the Holy Place if he entered a Scotch Presbyterian, or a Dutch Calvinist, place of worship. Rome does not fight against the Daily Sacrifice, and endeavor to abolish it; that has been rather the labor of so-called Church Reformers, who with the suppression of the doctrine of Eucharistic Sacrifice and Sacramental Adoration have well nigh obliterated all notion of worship to be addressed to the God-Man. Rome does not deny the power of the godliness of which she makes show, but insists on that power with no broken accents. It is rather in other communities, where authority is flung aside, and any man is permitted to believe or reject what he likes, that we must look for the leaven of the Antichristian spirit at work.

It is evident that this spirit will infect the Church, and especially those in place of authority therein; so that the elect will have to wrestle against both "principalities and powers" in the state, and also "spiritual wickedness in the high places" of the Church. Perhaps it will be this feeling of antagonism between the inferior orders and the highest which will throw the Bishops into the arms of the state, and establish that unholy alliance which will be cemented for the purpose of oppressing all who hold the truth in sincerity, who are definite in their dogmatic statements of Christ's having been manifested in the flesh, who labor to establish the Daily Sacrifice, and offer in every place the pure offering spoken of by Malachi. Perhaps it was in anticipation of this, that ancient mystical interpreters explained the scene at the well in Midian as having reference to the last times.

The Church, like the daughters of Reuel, comes to the Well of living waters to water her parched flock; whereupon the shepherds—her chief pastors—arise and strive with her. "Fear not, O flock, fear not, O daughter!" exclaims the commentator; "thy true Moses is seated on the well, and He will arise out of His resting-place, and will with His own hand smite the shepherds, and water the flock." Let the sheep be in barren and dry pastures,—so long the shepherds strive not; let the sheep pant and die,—so long the shepherds show no signs of irritation; but let the Church approach the limpid well of life, and at once her prelates will, in the latter days, combine "to strive" with her, and keep back the flock from the reviving streams.

In the time of Antichrist the Church will be divided: one portion will hold to the world-power, the other will seek out the old paths, and cling to the only true Guide. The high places will be filled with unbelievers in the Incarnation, and the Church will be in a condition of the utmost spiritual degradation, but enjoying the highest State patronage. The religion in favor will be one of morality, but not of dogma; and the Man of Sin will be able to promulgate his doctrine, according to St. Anselm, through his great eloquence and wisdom, his vast learning and mightiness in the Holy Scriptures, which he will wrest to the overthrowing of dogma. He will be liberal in bribes, for he will be of unbounded wealth; he will be capable of performing great "signs and wonders," so as "to deceive—the very elect;" and at the last, he will tear the moral veil from his countenance, and a monster of impiety and cruelty, he will inaugurate that awful persecution, which is to last for three years and a half, and to excel in horror all the persecutions that have gone before.

In that terrible season of confusion faith will be all but extinguished. "When the Son of Man cometh, shall He find faith on the earth?" asks our Blessed Lord, as though expecting the answer, No; and then, says Marchantius, the vessel of the Church will disappear in the foam of that boiling deep of infidelity, and be hidden in the blackness of that storm of destruction which sweeps over the earth. The sun shall "be darkened, and the moon shall not give her light, and the stars shall fall from heaven;" the sun of faith shall have gone out; the moon, the Church, shall not give her light, being turned into blood, through stress of persecution; and the stars, the great ecclesiastical dignitaries, shall fall into apostasy. But still the Church will remain unwrecked, she will weather the storm; still will she come forth "beautiful as the moon, terrible as an army with banners;" for after the lapse of those three and a half years, Christ will descend to avenge the blood of the saints, by destroying Antichrist and the world-power.

Such is a brief sketch of the scriptural doctrine of Antichrist as held by the early and mediæval Church. Let us now see to what myths it gave rise among the vulgar and the imaginative. Rabanus Maurus, in his work on the life of Antichrist, gives a full account of the miracles he will perform; he tells us that the Man-fiend will heal the sick, raise the dead, restore sight to the blind, hearing to the deaf, speech to the dumb; he will raise storms and calm them, will remove mountains, make trees flourish or wither at a word. He will rebuild the temple at Jerusalem, and making the Holy City the great capital of the world. Popular opinion added that his vast wealth would be obtained from hidden treasures, which are now being concealed by the demons for his use. Various possessed persons, when interrogated, announced that such was the case, and that the amount of buried gold was vast.

"In the year 1599," says Canon Moreau, a contemporary historian, "a rumor circulated with prodigious rapidity through Europe, that Antichrist had been born at Babylon, and that already the Jews of that part were hurrying to receive and recognize him as their Messiah. The news came from Italy and Germany, and extended to Spain, England, and other Western kingdoms, troubling many people, even the most discreet; however, the learned gave it no credence, saying that the signs predicted in Scripture to precede that event were not yet accomplished, and among other that the Roman empire was not yet abolished.... Others said that, as for the signs, the majority had already appeared to the best of their knowledge, and with regard to the rest, they might have taken place in distant regions without their having been made known to them; that the Roman empire existed but in name, and that the interpretation of the passage on which its destruction was predicted, might be incorrect; that for many centuries, the most learned and pious had believed in the near approach of Antichrist, some believing that he had already come, on account of the persecutions which had fallen on the Christians; others, on account of fires, or eclipses, or earthquakes.... Every one was in excitement; some declared that the news must be correct, others believed nothing about it, and the agitation became so excessive, that Henry IV., who was then on the throne, was compelled by edict to forbid any mention of the subject."

The report spoken of by Moreau gained additional

confirmation from the announcement made by an exorcised demoniac, that in 1600, the Man of Sin had been born in the neighborhood of Paris, of a Jewess, named Blanchefleure, who had conceived by Satan. The child had been baptized at the Sabbath of Sorcerers; and a witch, under torture, acknowledged that she had rocked the infant Antichrist on her knees, and she averred that he had claws on his feet, wore no shoes, and spoke all languages.

In 1623 appeared the following startling announcement, which obtained an immense circulation among the lower orders: "We, brothers of the Order of St. John of Jerusalem, in the Isle of Malta, have received letters from our spies, who are engaged in our service in the country of Babylon, now possessed by the Grand Turk; by the which letters we are advertised, that, on the 1st of May, in the year of our Lord 1623, a child was born in the town of Bourydot, otherwise called Calka, near Babylon, of the which child the mother is a very aged woman, of race unknown, called Fort-Juda: of the father nothing is known. The child is dusky, has pleasant mouth and eyes, teeth pointed like those of a cat, ears large, stature by no means exceeding that of other children; the said child, incontinent on his birth, walked and talked perfectly well. His speech is comprehended by every one, admonishing the people that he is the true Messiah, and the son of God, and that in him all must believe. Our spies also swear and protest that they have seen the said child with their own eyes; and they add, that, on the occasion of his nativity, there appeared marvellous signs in heaven, for at full noon the sun lost its brightness, and was for some time obscured." This is followed by a list of other signs appearing, the most remarkable being a swarm of flying serpents, and a shower of precious stones.

According to Sebastian Michaeliz, in his history of the possessed of Flanders, on the authority of the exorcised demons, we learn that Antichrist is to be a son of Beelzebub, who will accompany his offspring under the form of a bird, with four feet and a bull's head; that he will torture Christians with the same tortures with which the lost souls are racked; that he will be able to fly, speak all languages, and will have any number of names.

We find that Antichrist is known to the Mussulmans as well as to Christians. Lane, in his edition of the "Arabian Nights," gives some curious details on Moslem ideas regarding him. According to these, Antichrist will overrun the earth, mounted on an ass, and followed by 40,000 Jews; his empire will last forty days, whereof the first day will be a year long, the duration of the second will be a month, that of the third a week, the others being of their usual length. He will devastate the whole world, leaving Mecca and Medina alone in security, as these holy cities will be guarded by angelic legions. Christ at last will descend to earth, and in a great battle will destroy the Man-devil.

Several writers, of different denominations, no less superstitious than the common people, connected the apparition of Antichrist with the fable of Pope Joan, which obtained such general credence at one time, but which modern criticism has at length succeeded in excluding from history.

Perhaps the earliest writer to mention Pope Joan is Marianus Scotus, who in his chronicle inserts the following passage: "A. D. 854, Lotharii 14, Joanna, a woman, succeeded Leo, and reigned two years, five months, and four days." Marianus Scotus died A. D. 1086. Sigebert de Gemblours (d. 5th Oct., 1112) inserts the same story in his valuable chronicle, copying from an interpolated passage in the work of Anastasius the librarian. His words are, "It is reported that this John was a female, and that she conceived by one of her servants. The Pope, becoming pregnant, gave birth to a child; wherefore some do not number her among the Pontiffs." Hence the story spread among the mediæval chroniclers, who were great plagiarists. Otto of Frisingen and Gotfrid of Viterbo mention the Lady-Pope in their histories, and Martin Polonus gives details as follows: "After Leo IV., John Anglus, a native of Metz, reigned two years, five months, and four days. And the pontificate was vacant for a month. He died in Rome. He is related to have been a female, and, when a girl, to have accompanied her sweetheart in male costume to Athens; there she advanced in various sciences, and none could be found to equal her. So, after having studied for three years in Rome, she had great masters for her pupils and hearers. And when there arose a high opinion in the city of her virtue and knowledge, she was unanimously elected Pope. But during her papacy she became in the family way by a familiar. Not knowing the time of birth, as she was on her way from St. Peter's to the Lateran she had a painful delivery, between the Coliseum and St. Clement's Church, in the street. Having died after, it is said that she was buried on the spot; and therefore the Lord Pope always turns aside from that way, and it is supposed by some out of detestation for what happened there. Nor on that account is she placed in the catalogue of the Holy Pontiffs, not only on account of her sex, but also because of the horribleness of the circumstance."

Certainly a story at all scandalous crescit eundo.

William Ocham alludes to the story, and John Huss, only too happy to believe it, provides the lady with a name, and asserts that she was baptized Agnes, or, as he will have it with a strong aspirate, Hagnes. Others, however, insist upon her name having been Gilberta; and some stout Germans, not relishing the notion of her being a daughter of Fatherland, palm her off on England. As soon as we arrive at Reformation times, the German and French Protestants fasten on the story with the utmost avidity, and add sweet little touches of their own, and draw conclusions galling enough to the Roman See, illustrating their accounts with wood engravings vigorous and graphic, but hardly decent. One of these represents the event in a peculiarly startling manner. The procession of bishops, with the Host and tapers, is sweeping along, when suddenly the cross-bearer before the triple-crowned and vested Pope starts aside to witness the unexpected arrival. This engraving, which it is quite impossible for me to reproduce, is in a curious little book, entitled "Puerperium Johannis Papæ 8, 1530."

The following jingling record of the event is from the Rhythmical Vitæ Pontificum of Gulielmus Jacobus of Egmonden, a work never printed. This fragment is preserved in "Wolfii Lectionum Memorabilium centenarii, XVI.:"—

"Priusquàm reconditur Sergius, vocatur
Ad summam, qui dicitur Johannes, huic addatur
Anglicus, Moguntia iste procreatur.
Qui, ut dat sententia, fœminis aptatur
Sexu: quod sequentia monstrant, breviatur,
Hæc vox: nam prolixius chronica procedunt.

> Ista, de qua brevius dicta minus lædunt.
> Huic erat amasius, ut scriptores credunt.
> Patria relinquitur Moguntia,
> Græcorum Studiosè petitur schola.
> Pòst doctorum Hæc doctrix efficitur Romæ legens: horum
> Hæc auditu fungitur loquens. Hinc prostrato
> Summo hæc eligitur: sexu exaltato
> Quandoque negligitur. Fatur quòd hæc nato
> Per servum conficitur. Tempore gignendi
> Ad processum equus scanditur, vice flendi,
> Papa cadit, panditur improbis ridendi
> Norma, puer nascitur in vico Clementis,
> Colossœum jungitur. Corpus parentis
> In eodem traditur sepulturæ gentis,
> Faturque scriptoribus, quòd Papa præfato,
> Vico senioribus transiens amato
> Congruo ductoribus sequitur negato
> Loco, quo Ecclesia partu denigratur,
> Quamvis inter spacia Pontificum ponatur,
> Propter sexum."

Stephen Blanch, in his "Urbis Romæ Mirabilia," says that an angel of heaven appeared to Joan before the event, and asked her to choose whether she would prefer burning eternally in hell, or having her confinement in public; with sense which does her credit, she chose the latter. The Protestant writers were not satisfied that the father of the unhappy baby should have been a servant: some made him a Cardinal, and others the devil himself. According to an eminent Dutch minister, it is immaterial whether the child be fathered on Satan or a monk; at all events, the former took a lively interest in the youthful Antichrist, and, on the occasion of his birth, was seen and heard fluttering overhead, crowing and chanting in an unmusical voice the Sibylline verses announcing the birth of the Arch-persecutor: —

> "Papa pater patrum, Papissæ pandito partum
> Et tibi tunc eadem de corpore quando recedam!"

which lines, as being perhaps the only ones known to be of diabolic composition, are deserving of preservation.

The Reformers, in order to reconcile dates, were put to the somewhat perplexing necessity of moving Pope Joan to their own times, or else of giving to the youthful Antichrist an age of seven hundred years.

It must be allowed that the accouchement of a Pope in full pontificals, during a solemn procession, was a prodigy not likely to occur more than once in the world's history, and was certain to be of momentous import.

It will be seen by the curious woodcut reproduced as frontispiece from Baptista Mantuanus, that he consigned Pope Joan to the jaws of hell, notwithstanding her choice. The verses accompanying this picture are:—

> "Hic pendebat adhuc sexum mentita virile
> Fœmina, cui triplici Phrygiam diademate mitram
> Extollebat apex: et pontificalis adulter."

It need hardly be stated that the whole story of Pope Joan is fabulous, and rests on not the slightest historical foundation. It was probably a Greek invention to throw discredit on the papal hierarchy, first circulated more than two hundred years after the date of the supposed Pope. Even Martin Polonus (A. D. 1282), who is the first to give the details, does so merely on popular report.

The great champions of the myth were the Protestants of the sixteenth century, who were thoroughly unscrupulous in distorting history and suppressing facts, so long as they could make a point. A paper war was waged upon the subject, and finally the whole story was proved conclusively to be utterly destitute of historical truth. A melancholy example of the blindness of party feeling and prejudice is seen in Mosheim, who assumes the truth of the ridiculous story, and gravely inserts it in his "Ecclesiastical History." "Between Leo IV., who died 855, and Benedict III., a woman, who concealed her sex and assumed the name of John, it is said, opened her way to the Pontifical throne by her learning and genius, and governed the Church for a time. She is commonly called the Papess Joan. During the five subsequent centuries the witnesses to this extraordinary event are without number; nor did any one, prior to the Reformation by Luther, regard the thing as either incredible or disgraceful to the Church." Such are Mosheim's words, and I give them as a specimen of the credit which is due to his opinion. The "Ecclesiastical History" he wrote is full of perversions of the plainest facts, and that under our notice is but one out of many. "During the five centuries after her reign," he says, "the witnesses to the story are innumerable." Now, for two centuries there is not an allusion to be found to the events. The only passage which can be found is a universally acknowledged interpolation of the "Lives of the Popes," by Anastasius Bibliothecarius; and this interpolation is stated in the first printed edition by Busæus, Mogunt. 1602, to be only found in two MS. copies.

From Marianus Scotus or Sigebert de Gemblours the story passed into other chronicles totidem verbis, and generally with hesitation and an expression of doubt in its accuracy. Martin Polonus is the first to give the particulars, some four hundred and twenty years after the reign of the fabulous Pope.

Mosheim is false again in asserting that no one prior to the Reformation regarded the thing as either incredible or disgraceful. This is but of a piece with his malignity and disregard for truth, whenever he can hit the Catholic Church hard. Bart. Platina, in his "Lives of the Popes," written before Luther was born, after relating the story, says, "These things which I relate are popular reports, but derived from uncertain and obscure authors, which I have therefore inserted briefly and baldly, lest I should seem to omit obstinately and pertinaciously what most people assert." Thus the facts were justly doubted by Platina on the legitimate grounds that they rested on popular gossip, and not on reliable history. Marianus Scotus, the first to relate the story, died in 1086. He was a monk of St. Martin of Cologne, then of Fulda, and lastly of St. Alban's, at Metz. How could he have obtained reliable information, or seen documents upon which to ground the assertion? Again, his chronicle has suffered severely from interpolations in numerous places, and there is reason to believe that the Pope-Joan passage is itself a late interpolation.

If so, we are reduced to Sigebert de Gemblours (d. 1112), placing two centuries and a half between him and the event he records, and his chronicle may have been tampered with.

The historical discrepancies are sufficiently glaring to make the story more than questionable.

Leo IV. died on the 17th July, 855; and Benedict III. was consecrated on the 1st September in the same year; so that it is impossible to insert between their pontificates a reign of two years, five months, and four days. It is, however, true that there was an antipope elected upon the death of Leo, at the instance of the Emperor Louis; but his name was Anastasius. This man possessed himself of the palace of the Popes, and obtained the incarceration of Benedict. However, his supporters almost immediately deserted him, and Benedict assumed the pontificate. The reign of Benedict was only for two years and a half, so that Anastasius cannot be the supposed Joan; nor do we hear of any charge brought against him to the effect of his being a woman. But the stout partisans of the Pope-Joan tale assert, on the authority of the "Annales Augustani,"[29] and some other, but late authorities, that the female Pope was John VIII., who consecrated Louis II. of France, and Ethelwolf of England. Here again is confusion. Ethelwolf sent Alfred to Rome in 853, and the youth received regal unction from the hands of Leo IV. In 855 Ethelwolf visited Rome, it is true, but was not consecrated by the existing Pope, whilst Charles the Bald was anointed by John VIII. in 875. John VIII. was a Roman, son of Gundus, and an archdeacon of the Eternal City. He assumed the triple crown in 872, and reigned till December 18, 882. John took an active part in the troubles of the Church under the incursions of the Sarasins, and 325 letters of his are extant, addressed to the princes and prelates of his day.

Any one desirous of pursuing this examination into the untenable nature of the story may find an excellent summary of the arguments used on both sides in Gieseler, "Lehrbuch," &c., Cunningham's trans., vol. ii. pp. 20, 21, or in Bayle, "Dictionnaire," tom. iii. art. Papesse.

---

[29] These Annals were written in 1135.

The arguments in favor of the myth may be seen in Spanheim, "Exercit. de Papa Fœmina," Opp. tom. ii. p. 577, or in Lenfant, "Histoire de la Papesse Jeanne," La Haye, 1736, 2 vols. 12mo.

The arguments on the other side may be had in "Allatii Confutatio Fabulæ de Johanna Papissa," Colon. 1645; in Le Quien, "Oriens Christianus," tom. iii. p. 777; and in the pages of the Lutheran Huemann, "Sylloge Diss. Sacras.," tom. i. par. ii. p. 352.

The final development of this extraordinary story, under the delicate fingers of the German and French Protestant controversialists, may not prove uninteresting.

Joan was the daughter of an English missionary, who left England to preach the Gospel to the recently converted Saxons. She was born at Engelheim, and according to different authors she was christened Agnes, Gerberta, Joanna, Margaret, Isabel, Dorothy, or Jutt—the last must have been a nickname surely! She early distinguished herself for genius and love of letters. A young monk of Fulda having conceived for her a violent passion, which she returned with ardor, she deserted her parents, dressed herself in male attire, and in the sacred precincts of Fulda divided her affections between the youthful monk and the musty books of the monastic library. Not satisfied with the restraints of conventual life, nor finding the library sufficiently well provided with books of abstruse science, she eloped with her young man, and after visiting England, France, and Italy, she brought him to Athens, where she addicted herself with unflagging devotion to her literary pursuits. Wearied out by his journey, the monk expired in the arms of the blue-stocking who had influenced his life for evil, and the young lady of so many aliases was for a while inconsolable. She left Athens and repaired to Rome. There she opened a school and acquired such a reputation for learning and feigned sanctity, that, on the death of Leo IV., she was unanimously elected Pope. For two years and five months, under the name of John VIII., she filled the papal chair with reputation, no one suspecting her sex. But having taken a fancy to one of the cardinals, by him she became pregnant. At length arrived the time of Rogation processions. Whilst passing the street between the amphitheatre and St. Clement's, she was seized with violent pains, fell to the ground amidst the crowd, and, whilst her attendants ministered to her, was delivered of a son. Some say the child and mother died on the spot, some that she survived but was incarcerated, some that the child was spirited away to be the Antichrist of the last days. A marble monument representing the papess with her baby was erected on the spot, which was declared to be accursed to all ages.

I have little doubt myself that Pope Joan is an impersonification of the great whore of Revelation, seated on the seven hills, and is the popular expression of the idea prevalent from the twelfth to the sixteenth centuries, that the mystery of iniquity was somehow working in the papal court. The scandal of the Antipopes, the utter worldliness and pride of others, the spiritual fornication with the kings of the earth, along with the words of Revelation prophesying the advent of an adulterous woman who should rule over the imperial city, and her connection with Antichrist, crystallized into this curious myth, much as the floating uncertainty as to the signification of our Lord's words, "There be some standing here which shall not taste of death till they see the kingdom of God," condensed into the myth of the Wandering Jew.

The literature connected with Antichrist is voluminous. I need only specify some of the most curious works which have appeared on the subject. St. Hippolytus and Rabanus Maurus have been already alluded to. Commodianus wrote "Carmen Apologeticum adversus Gentes," which has been published by Dom Pitra in his "Spicilegium Solesmense," with an introduction containing Jewish and Christian traditions relating to Antichrist. "De Turpissima Conceptione, Nativitate, et aliis Præsagiis Diaboliciis illius Turpissimi Hominis Antichristi," is the title of a strange little volume published by Lenoir in A. D. 1500, containing rude yet characteristic woodcuts, representing the birth, life, and death of the Man of Sin, each picture accompanied by French verses in explanation. An equally remarkable illustrated work on Antichrist is the famous "Liber de Antichristo," a blockbook of an early date. It is in twenty-seven folios, and is excessively rare. Dibdin has reproduced three of the plates in his "Bibliotheca Spenseriana," and Falckenstein has given full details of the work in his "Geschichte der Buchdruckerkunst."

There is an Easter miracle-play of the twelfth century, still extant, the subject of which is the "Life and Death of Antichrist." More curious still is the "Farce de l'Antéchrist et de Trois Femmes"—a composition of the sixteenth century, when that mysterious personage occupied all brains. The farce consists in a scene at a fish-stall, with three good ladies quarrelling over some fish. Antichrist steps in,—for no particular reason that one can see,—upsets fish and fish-women, sets them fighting, and skips off the stage. The best book on Antichrist, and that most full of learning and judgment, is Malvenda's great work in two folio volumes, "De Antichristo, libri xii." Lyons, 1647.

For the fable of the Pope Joan, see J. Lenfant, "Histoire de la Papesse Jeanne." La Haye, 1736, 2 vols. 12mo. "Allatii Confutatio Fabulæ de Johanna Papissa." Colon. 1645.

THE MAN IN THE MOON

EVERY one knows that the moon is inhabited by a man with a bundle of sticks on his back, who has been exiled thither for many centuries, and who is so far off that he is beyond the reach of death.

He has once visited this earth, if the nursery rhyme is to be credited, when it asserts that—

> "The Man in the Moon
> Came down too soon,
> And asked his way to Norwich;"

but whether he ever reached that city, the same authority does not state.

The story as told by nurses is, that this man was found by Moses gathering sticks on a Sabbath, and that, for this crime, he was doomed to reside in the moon till the end of all things; and they refer to Numbers xv. 32-36:—

"And while the children of Israel were in the wilderness, they found a man that gathered sticks upon the Sabbath day. And they that found him gathering sticks brought him unto Moses and Aaron, and unto all the congregation. And they put him in ward, because it was not declared what should be done to him. And the Lord said unto Moses, The man shall be surely put to death: all the congregation shall stone him with stones without the camp. And all the congregation brought him without the camp, and stoned him with stones till he died."

Of course, in the sacred writings there is no allusion to the moon.

The German tale is as follows:—

Ages ago there went one Sunday morning an old man into the wood to hew sticks. He cut a fagot and slung it on a stout staff, cast it over his shoulder, and began to trudge home with his burden. On his way he met a handsome man in Sunday suit, walking towards the Church; this man stopped and asked the fagot-bearer, "Do you know that this is Sunday on earth, when all must rest from their labors?"

"Sunday on earth, or Monday in heaven, it is all one to me!" laughed the wood-cutter.

"Then bear your bundle forever," answered the stranger; "and as you value not Sunday on earth, yours shall be a perpetual Moonday in heaven; and you shall stand for eternity in the moon, a warning to all Sabbath-breakers." Thereupon the stranger vanished, and the man was caught up with his stock and his fagot into the moon, where he stands yet.

The superstition seems to be old in Germany, for the full moon is spoken of as wadel, or wedel, a fagot. Tobler relates the story thus: "An arma mā ket alawel am Sonnti holz ufglesa. Do hedem der liebe Gott dwahl gloh, öb er lieber wott ider sonn verbrenna oder im mo verfrura, do willer lieber inn mo ihi. Dromm siedma no jetz an ma im mo inna, wenns wedel ist. Er hed a püscheli uffem rogga."[30] That is to say, he was given the choice of burning in the sun, or of freezing in the moon; he chose the latter; and now at full moon he is to be seen seated with his bundle of fagots on his back.

In Schaumburg-Lippe,[31] the story goes, that a man and a woman stand in the moon, the man because he strewed brambles and thorns on the church path, so as to hinder people from attending Mass on Sunday morning; the woman because she made butter on that day. The man carries his bundle of thorns, the woman her butter-tub. A similar tale is told in Swabia and in Marken. Fischart[32] says, that there "is to be seen in the moon a manikin who stole wood;" and Prætorius, in his description of the world,[33] that "superstitious people assert that the black flecks in the moon are a man who gathered wood on a Sabbath, and is therefore turned into stone."

The Dutch household myth is, that the unhappy man was caught stealing vegetables. Dante calls him Cain:—

---

30 Tobler, Appenz. Sprachsbuch, 20.
31 Wolf, Zeitschrift für Deut. Myth. i. 168.
32 Fischart, Garg. 130.
33 Prætorius, i. 447.

"... Now doth Cain with fork of thorns confine,
On either hemisphere, touching the wave
Beneath the towers of Seville. Yesternight
The moon was round."

Hell, cant. xx.

And again,—

"... Tell, I pray thee, whence the gloomy spots
Upon this body, which below on earth
Give rise to talk of Cain in fabling quaint?"

Paradise, cant. ii.

Chaucer, in the "Testament of Cresside," adverts to the man in the moon, and attributes to him the same idea of theft. Of Lady Cynthia, or the moon, he says,—

"Her gite was gray and full of spottis blake,
And on her brest a chorle painted ful even,
Bering a bush of thornis on his backe,
Whiche for his theft might clime so ner the heaven."

Ritson, among his "Ancient Songs," gives one extracted from a manuscript of the time of Edward II., on the Man in the Moon, but in very obscure language. The first verse, altered into more modern orthography, runs as follows:—

"Man in the Moon stand and stit,
On his bot-fork his burden he beareth,
It is much wonder that he do na doun slit,
For doubt lest he fall he shudd'reth and shivereth.

* * * * *

"When the frost freezes must chill he bide,
The thorns be keen his attire so teareth,
Nis no wight in the world there wot when he syt,
Ne bote it by the hedge what weeds he weareth."

Alexander Necham, or Nequam, a writer of the twelfth century, in commenting on the dispersed shadows in the moon, thus alludes to the vulgar belief: "Nonne novisti quid vulgus vocet rusticum in luna portantem spinas? Unde quidam vulgariter loquens ait:—

> "Rusticus in Luna,
> Quem sarcina deprimit una
> Monstrat per opinas
> Nulli prodesse rapinas,"

which may be translated thus: "Do you know what they call the rustic in the moon, who carries the fagot of sticks?" So that one vulgarly speaking says,—

> "See the rustic in the Moon,
> How his bundle weighs him down;
> Thus his sticks the truth reveal,
> It never profits man to steal."

Shakspeare refers to the same individual in his "Midsummer Night's Dream." Quince the carpenter, giving directions for the performance of the play of "Pyramus and Thisbe," orders: "One must come in with a bush of thorns and a lantern, and say he comes in to disfigure, or to present, the person of Moonshine." And the enacter of this part says, "All I have to say is, to tell you that the lantern is the moon; I the man in the moon; this thorn-bush my thorn-bush; and this dog my dog."

Also "Tempest," Act 2, Scene 2:—

> "Cal. Hast thou not dropt from heaven?
> "Steph. Out o' th' moon, I do assure thee. I was the
> man in th' moon when time was.
> "Cal. I have seen thee in her; and I do adore thee. My
> mistress showed me thee, and thy dog, and thy bush."

The dog I have myself had pointed out to me by an old

Devonshire crone. If popular superstition places a dog in the moon, it puts a lamb in the sun; for in the same county it is said that those who see the sun rise on Easter-day, may behold in the orb the lamb and flag.

I believe this idea of locating animals in the two great luminaries of heaven to be very ancient, and to be a relic of a primeval superstition of the Aryan race.

There is an ancient pictorial representation of our friend the Sabbath-breaker in Gyffyn Church, near Conway. The roof of the chancel is divided into compartments, in four of which are the Evangelistic symbols, rudely, yet effectively painted. Besides these symbols is delineated in each compartment an orb of heaven. The sun, the moon, and two stars, are placed at the feet of the Angel, the Bull, the Lion, and the Eagle. The representation of the moon is as below; in the disk is the

conventional man with his bundle of sticks, but without the dog. There is also a curious seal appended to a deed preserved in the Record Office, dated the 9th year of Edward the Third (1335), bearing the man in the moon as its device. The deed is one of conveyance of a messuage, barn, and four acres of ground, in the parish of Kingston-on-Thames, from Walter de Grendesse, clerk, to Margaret his mother. On the seal we see the man carrying his sticks, and the moon surrounds him. There are also a couple of stars added, perhaps to show that he is in the sky. The legend on the seal reads:—

"Te Waltere docebo

cur spinas phebo

gero,"

which may be translated, "I will teach thee, Walter, why I carry thorns in the moon."

The general superstition with regard to the spots in the moon may briefly be summed up thus: A man is located in the moon; he is a thief or Sabbath-breaker;[34] he has a pole over his shoulder, from which is suspended a bundle of sticks or thorns. In some places a woman is believed to accompany him, and she has a butter-tub with her; in other localities she is replaced by a dog.

The belief in the Moon-man seems to exist among the natives of British Columbia; for I read in one of Mr. Duncan's letters to the Church Missionary Society, "One very dark night I was told that there was a moon to see on the beach. On going to see, there was an illuminated disk, with the figure of a man upon it. The water was then very low, and one of the conjuring parties had lit up this disk at the water's edge. They had made it of wax, with great exactness, and presently it was at full. It was an imposing sight. Nothing could be seen around it; but the Indians suppose that the medicine party are then holding converse with the man in the moon.... After a short

---

[34] Hebel, in his charming poem on the Man in the Moon, in "Allemanische Gedichte," makes him both thief and Sabbath-breaker.

107

time the moon waned away, and the conjuring party returned whooping to their house."

Now let us turn to Scandinavian mythology, and see what we learn from that source.

Mâni, the moon, stole two children from their parents, and carried them up to heaven. Their names were Hjuki and Bil. They had been drawing water from the well Byrgir, in the bucket Sœgr, suspended from the pole Simul, which they bore upon their shoulders. These children, pole, and bucket were placed in heaven, "where they could be seen from earth." This refers undoubtedly to the spots in the moon; and so the Swedish peasantry explain these spots to this day, as representing a boy and a girl bearing a pail of water between them. Are we not reminded at once of our nursery rhyme—

> "Jack and Jill went up a hill
> To fetch a pail of water;
> Jack fell down, and broke his crown,
> And Jill came tumbling after"?

This verse, which to us seems at first sight nonsense, I have no hesitation in saying has a high antiquity, and refers to the Eddaic Hjuki and Bil. The names indicate as much. Hjuki, in Norse, would be pronounced Juki, which would readily become Jack; and Bil, for the sake of euphony, and in order to give a female name to one of the children, would become Jill.

The fall of Jack, and the subsequent fall of Jill, simply represent the vanishing of one moon-spot after another, as the moon wanes.

But the old Norse myth had a deeper signification than merely an explanation of the moon-spots.

Hjuki is derived from the verb jakka, to heap or pile together, to assemble and increase; and Bil from bila, to break up or dissolve. Hjuki and Bil, therefore, signify nothing more than the waxing and waning of the moon, and the water they are represented as bearing signifies the fact that the rainfall depends on the phases of the moon. Waxing and waning were individualized, and the meteorological fact of the connection of the rain with the moon was represented by the children as water-bearers.

But though Jack and Jill became by degrees dissevered in the popular mind from the moon, the original myth went through a fresh phase, and exists still under a new form. The Norse superstition attributed theft to the moon, and the vulgar soon began to believe that the figure they saw in the moon was the thief. The lunar specks certainly may be made to resemble one figure, and only a lively imagination can discern two. The girl soon dropped out of popular mythology, the boy oldened into a venerable man, he retained his pole, and the bucket was transformed into the thing he had stolen—sticks or vegetables. The theft was in some places exchanged for Sabbath-breaking, especially among those in Protestant countries who were acquainted with the Bible story of the stick-gatherer.

The Indian superstition is worth examining, because of the connection existing between Indian and European mythology, on account of our belonging to the same Aryan stock.

According to a Buddhist legend, Sâkyamunni himself, in one of his earlier stages of existence, was a hare, and lived in friendship with a fox and an ape. In order to test the virtue of the Bodhisattwa, Indra came to the friends, in the form of an old man, asking for food. Hare, ape, and fox went forth in quest of victuals for their guest. The two latter returned from their foraging expedition successful, but the hare had found nothing. Then, rather than that he should treat the old man with inhospitality, the hare had a fire kindled, and cast himself into the flames, that he might himself become food for his guest. In reward for this act of self-sacrifice, Indra carried the hare to heaven, and placed him in the moon.[35]

Here we have an old man and a hare in connection with the lunar planet, just as in Shakspeare we have a fagot-bearer and a dog.

The fable rests upon the name of the moon in Sanskrit, çaçin, or "that marked with the hare;" but whether the belief in the spots

---

[35] "Mémoires ... par Hjouen Thsang, traduits du Chinois par Stanislas Julien," i. 375. Upham, "Sacred Books of Ceylon," iii. 309.

taking the shape of a hare gave the name çaçin to the moon, or the lunar name çaçin originated the belief, it is impossible for us to say.

Grounded upon this myth is the curious story of "The Hare and the Elephant," in the "Pantschatantra," an ancient collection of Sanskrit fables. It will be found as the first tale in the third book. I have room only for an outline of the story.

THE CRAFTY HARE

In a certain forest lived a mighty elephant, king of a herd, Toothy by name. On a certain occasion there was a long drought, so that pools, tanks, swamps, and lakes were dried up. Then the elephants sent out exploring parties in search of water. A young one discovered an extensive lake surrounded with trees, and teeming with water-fowl. It went by the name of the Moon-lake. The elephants, delighted at the prospect of having an inexhaustible supply of water, marched off to the spot, and found their most sanguine hopes realized. Round about the lake, in the sandy soil, were innumerable hare warrens; and as the herd of elephants trampled on the ground, the hares were severely injured, their homes broken down, their heads, legs, and backs crushed beneath the ponderous feet of the monsters of the forest. As soon as the herd had withdrawn, the hares assembled, some halting, some dripping with blood, some bearing the corpses of their cherished infants, some with piteous tales of ruination in their houses, all with tears streaming from their eyes, and wailing forth, "Alas, we are lost! The elephant-herd will return, for there is no water elsewhere, and that will be the death of all of us."

But the wise and prudent Longear volunteered to drive the herd away; and he succeeded in this manner: Longear went to the elephants, and having singled out their king, he addressed him as follows:—

"Ha, ha! bad elephant! what brings you with such thoughtless frivolity to this strange lake? Back with you at once!"

When the king of the elephants heard this, he asked in astonishment, "Pray, who are you?"

"I," replied Longear,—"I am Vidschajadatta by name; the hare who resides in the Moon. Now am I sent by his Excellency the Moon as an ambassador to you. I speak to you in the name of the Moon."

"Ahem! Hare," said the elephant, somewhat staggered; "and what message have you brought me from his Excellency the Moon?"

"You have this day injured several hares. Are you not aware that they are the subjects of me? If you value your life, venture not near the lake again. Break my command, and I shall withdraw my beams from you at night, and your bodies will be consumed with perpetual sun."

The elephant, after a short meditation, said, "Friend! it is true that I have acted against the rights of the excellent Majesty of the Moon. I should wish to make an apology; how can I do so?"

The hare replied, "Come along with me, and I will show you."

The elephant asked, "Where is his Excellency at present?"

The other replied, "He is now in the lake, hearing the complaints of the maimed hares."

"If that be the case," said the elephant, humbly, "bring me to my lord, that I may tender him my submission."

So the hare conducted the king of the elephants to the edge of the lake, and showed him the reflection of the moon in the water, saying, "There stands our lord in the midst of the water, plunged in meditation; reverence him with devotion, and then depart with speed."

Thereupon the elephant poked his proboscis into the water, and muttered a fervent prayer. By so doing he set the water in agitation, so that the reflection of the moon was all of a quiver.

"Look!" exclaimed the hare; "his Majesty is trembling with rage at you!"

"Why is his supreme Excellency enraged with me?" asked the elephant.

"Because you have set the water in motion. Worship him, and then be off!"

The elephant let his ears droop, bowed his great head to the earth, and after having expressed in suitable terms his regret for having annoyed the Moon, and the hare dwelling in it, he vowed never to trouble the Moon-lake again. Then he departed, and the hares have ever since lived there unmolested.

THE MOUNTAIN OF VENUS

RAGGED, bald, and desolate, as though a curse rested upon it, rises the Hörselberg out of the rich and populous land between Eisenach and Gotha, looking, from a distance, like a huge stone sarcophagus—a sarcophagus in which rests in magical slumber, till the end of all things, a mysterious world of wonders.

High up on the north-west flank of the mountain, in a precipitous wall of rock, opens a cavern, called the Hörselloch, from the depths of which issues a muffled roar of water, as though a subterraneous stream were rushing over rapidly-whirling millwheels. "When I have stood alone on the ridge of the mountain," says Bechstein, "after having sought the chasm in vain, I have heard a mighty rush, like that of falling water, beneath my feet, and after scrambling down the scarp, have found myself— how, I never knew—in front of the cave." ("Sagenschatz des Thüringes-landes," 1835.)

In ancient days, according to the Thüringian Chronicles, bitter cries and long-drawn moans were heard issuing from this cavern; and at night, wild shrieks and the burst of diabolical laughter would ring from it over the vale, and fill the inhabitants with terror. It was supposed that this hole gave admittance to Purgatory; and the popular but faulty derivation of Hörsel was Höre, die Seele— Hark, the Souls!

But another popular belief respecting this mountain was, that in it Venus, the pagan Goddess of Love, held her court, in all the pomp and revelry of heathendom; and there were not a few who declared that they had seen fair forms of female beauty beckoning them from the mouth of the chasm, and that they had heard dulcet strains of music well up from the abyss above the thunder of the falling, unseen torrent. Charmed by the music, and allured by the spectral forms, various individuals had entered the cave, and none had returned, except the Tanhäuser, of whom more anon. Still does the Hörselberg go by the name of the Venusberg, a name frequently used in the middle ages, but without its locality being defined.

"In 1398, at midday, there appeared suddenly three great fires in the air, which presently ran together into one globe of flame, parted again, and finally sank into the Hörselberg," says the Thüringian Chronicle.

And now for the story of Tanhäuser.

A French knight was riding over the beauteous meadows in the Hörsel vale on his way to Wartburg, where the Landgrave Hermann was holding a gathering of minstrels, who were to contend in song for a prize.

Tanhäuser was a famous minnesinger, and all his lays were of love and of women, for his heart was full of passion, and that not of the purest and noblest description.

It was towards dusk that he passed the cliff in which is the Hörselloch, and as he rode by, he saw a white glimmering figure of matchless beauty standing before him, and beckoning him to her. He knew her at once, by her attributes and by her superhuman perfection, to be none other than Venus. As she spake to him, the sweetest strains of music floated in the air, a soft roseate light glowed around her, and nymphs of exquisite loveliness scattered roses at her feet. A thrill of passion ran through the veins of the minnesinger; and, leaving his horse, he followed the apparition. It led him up the mountain to the cave, and as it went flowers bloomed upon the soil, and a radiant track was left for Tanhäuser to follow. He entered the cavern, and descended to the palace of Venus in the heart of the mountain.

Seven years of revelry and debauch were passed, and the minstrel's heart began to feel a strange void. The beauty, the magnificence, the variety of the scenes in the pagan goddess's home, and all its heathenish pleasures, palled upon him, and he yearned for the pure fresh breezes of earth, one look up at the dark night sky spangled with stars, one glimpse of simple mountain-flowers, one tinkle of sheep-bells. At the same time his conscience began to reproach him, and he longed to make his peace with God. In vain did he entreat Venus to permit him to depart, and it was only when, in the bitterness of his grief, he called upon the Virgin-Mother, that a rift in the mountain-side appeared to him, and he stood again above ground.

How sweet was the morning air, balmy with the scent of hay, as it rolled up the mountain to him, and fanned his haggard cheek! How delightful to him was the cushion of moss and scanty grass after the downy couches of the palace of revelry below! He plucked the little heather-bells, and held them before him; the tears rolled from his eyes, and moistened his thin and wasted hands. He looked up at the soft blue sky and the newly-risen sun, and his heart overflowed. What were the golden, jewel-incrusted, lamp-lit vaults beneath to that pure dome of God's building!

The chime of a village church struck sweetly on his ear, satiated with Bacchanalian songs; and he hurried down the mountain to the church which called him. There he made his confession; but the priest, horror-struck at his recital, dared not give him absolution, but passed him on to another. And so he went from one to another, till at last he was referred to the Pope himself. To the Pope he went. Urban IV. then occupied the chair of St. Peter. To him Tanhäuser related the sickening story of his guilt, and prayed for absolution. Urban was a hard and stern man, and shocked at the immensity of the sin, he thrust the penitent indignantly from him, exclaiming, "Guilt such as thine can never, never be remitted. Sooner shall this staff in my hand grow green and blossom, than that God should pardon thee!"

Then Tanhäuser, full of despair, and with his soul darkened, went away, and returned to the only asylum open to him, the Venusberg. But lo! three days after he had gone, Urban discovered that his pastoral staff had put forth buds, and had burst into flower. Then he sent messengers after Tanhäuser, and they reached the Hörsel vale to hear that a wayworn man, with haggard brow and bowed head, had just entered the Hörselloch. Since then Tanhäuser has not been seen.

Such is the sad yet beautiful story of Tanhäuser. It is a very ancient myth Christianized, a wide-spread tradition localized. Originally heathen, it has been transformed, and has acquired new beauty by an infusion of Christianity. Scattered over Europe, it exists in various forms, but in none so graceful as that attached to the Hörselberg. There are, however, other Venusbergs in Germany; as, for instance, in Swabia, near Waldsee; another near Ufhausen, at no great distance from Freiburg (the same story is told of this Venusberg as of the Hörselberg); in Saxony there is a Venusberg not far from Wolkenstein. Paracelsus speaks of a Venusberg in Italy, referring to that in which Æneas Sylvius (Ep. 16) says Venus or a Sibyl resides, occupying a cavern, and assuming once a week the form of a serpent. Geiler v. Keysersperg, a quaint old preacher of the fifteenth century, speaks of the witches assembling on the Venusberg.

The story, either in prose or verse, has often been printed. Some of the earliest editions are the following:—

"Das Lied von dem Danhewser." Nürnberg, without date; the same, Nürnberg, 1515.—"Das Lyedt v. d. Thanheuser." Leyptzk, 1520.—"Das Lied v. d. Danheüser," reprinted by Bechstein, 1835.— "Das Lied vom edlen Tanheuser, Mons Veneris." Frankfort, 1614; Leipzig, 1668.—"Twe lede volgen Dat erste vain Danhüsser." Without date.—"Van heer Danielken." Tantwerpen, 1544.—A Danish version in "Nyerup, Danske Viser," No. VIII.

Let us now see some of the forms which this remarkable myth assumed in other countries. Every popular tale has its root, a root which may be traced among different countries, and though the accidents of the story may vary, yet the substance remains unaltered. It has been said that the common people never invent new story-radicals any more than we invent new word-roots; and this is perfectly true. The same story-root remains, but it is varied according to the temperament of the narrator or the exigencies of localization. The story-root of the Venusberg is this:—

> The underground folk seek union with human beings.
> α. A man is enticed into their abode, where he unites
> with a woman of the underground race.
> β. He desires to revisit the earth, and escapes.
> γ. He returns again to the region below.

Now, there is scarcely a collection of folk-lore which does not contain a story founded on this root. It appears in every branch of the Aryan family, and examples might be quoted from Modern Greek, Albanian, Neapolitan, French, German, Danish, Norwegian and Swedish, Icelandic, Scotch, Welsh, and other collections of popular tales. I have only space to mention some.

There is a Norse Tháttr of a certain Helgi Thorir's son, which is, in its present form, a production of the fourteenth century. Helgi and his brother Thorstein went on a cruise to Finnmark, or Lapland. They reached a ness, and found the land covered with forest. Helgi explored this forest, and lighted suddenly on a party of red-dressed women riding upon red horses. These ladies were beautiful and of troll race. One surpassed the others in beauty, and she was their mistress. They erected a tent and prepared a feast. Helgi observed that all their vessels were of silver and gold. The lady, who named herself Ingibjorg, advanced towards the Norseman, and invited him to live with her. He feasted and lived with the trolls for three days, and then returned to his ship, bringing with him two chests of silver and gold, which Ingibjorg had given him. He had been forbidden to mention where he had been and with whom; so he told no one whence he had obtained the chests. The ships sailed, and he returned home.

One winter's night Helgi was fetched away from home, in the midst of a furious storm, by two mysterious horsemen, and no one was able to ascertain for many years what had become of him, till the prayers of the king, Olaf, obtained his release, and then he was restored to his father and brother, but he was thenceforth blind. All the time of his absence he had been with the red-vested lady in her mysterious abode of Glœsisvellir.

The Scotch story of Thomas of Ercildoune is the same story. Thomas met with a strange lady, of elfin race, beneath Eildon Tree, who led him into the underground land, where he remained with her for seven years. He then returned to earth, still, however, remaining bound to come to his royal mistress whenever she should summon him. Accordingly, while Thomas was making merry with his friends in the Tower of Ercildoune, a person came running in, and told, with marks of fear and astonishment, that a hart and a hind had left the neighboring forest, and were parading the street of the village. Thomas instantly arose, left his house, and followed the animals into the forest, from which he never returned. According to popular belief, he still "drees his weird" in Fairy

Land, and is one day expected to revisit earth. (Scott, "Minstrelsy of the Scottish Border.") Compare with this the ancient ballad of Tamlane.

Debes relates that "it happened a good while since, when the burghers of Bergen had the commerce of the Faroe Isles, that there was a man in Serraade, called Jonas Soideman, who was kept by the spirits in a mountain during the space of seven years, and at length came out, but lived afterwards in great distress and fear, lest they should again take him away; wherefore people were obliged to watch him in the night." The same author mentions another young man who had been carried away, and after his return was removed a second time, upon the eve of his marriage.

Gervase of Tilbury says that "in Catalonia there is a lofty mountain, named Cavagum, at the foot of which runs a river with golden sands, in the vicinity of which there are likewise silver mines. This mountain is steep, and almost inaccessible. On its top, which is always covered with ice and snow, is a black and bottomless lake, into which if a stone be cast, a tempest suddenly arises; and near this lake is the portal of the palace of demons." He then tells how a young damsel was spirited in there, and spent seven years with the mountain spirits. On her return to earth she was thin and withered, with wandering eyes, and almost bereft of understanding.

A Swedish story is to this effect. A young man was on his way to his bride, when he was allured into a mountain by a beautiful elfin woman. With her he lived forty years, which passed as an hour; on his return to earth all his old friends and relations were dead, or had forgotten him, and finding no rest there, he returned to his mountain elf-land.

In Pomerania, a laborer's son, Jacob Dietrich of Rambin, was enticed away in the same manner.

There is a curious story told by Fordun in his "Scotichronicon," which has some interest in connection with the legend of the Tanhäuser. He relates that in the year 1050, a youth of noble birth had been married in Rome, and during the nuptial feast, being engaged in a game of ball, he took off his wedding-ring, and placed it on the finger of a statue of Venus. When he wished to resume it, he found that the stony hand had become clinched, so that it was impossible to remove the ring. Thenceforth he was haunted by the Goddess Venus, who constantly whispered in his ear, "Embrace me; I am Venus, whom you have wedded; I will never restore your ring." However, by the assistance of a priest, she was at length forced to give it up to its rightful owner.

The classic legend of Ulysses, held captive for eight years by the nymph Calypso in the Island of Ogygia, and again for one year by the enchantress Circe, contains the root of the same story of the Tanhäuser.

What may have been the significance of the primeval story-radical it is impossible for us now to ascertain; but the legend, as it shaped itself in the middle ages, is certainly indicative of the struggle between the new and the old faith.

We see thinly veiled in Tanhäuser the story of a man, Christian in name, but heathen at heart, allured by the attractions of paganism, which seems to satisfy his poetic instincts, and which gives full rein to his passions. But these excesses pall on him after a while, and the religion of sensuality leaves a great void in his breast.

He turns to Christianity, and at first it seems to promise all that he requires. But alas! he is repelled by its ministers. On all sides he is met by practice widely at variance with profession. Pride, worldliness, want of sympathy exist among those who should be the foremost to guide, sustain, and receive him. All the warm springs which gushed up in his broken heart are choked, his softened spirit is hardened again, and he returns in despair to bury his sorrows and drown his anxieties in the debauchery of his former creed.

A sad picture, but doubtless one very true.

FATALITY OF NUMBERS

THE laws governing numbers are so perplexing to the uncultivated mind, and the results arrived at by calculation are so astonishing, that it cannot be matter of surprise if superstition has attached itself to numbers.

But even to those who are instructed in numeration, there is much that is mysterious and unaccountable, much that only an advanced mathematician can explain to his own satisfaction. The neophyte sees the numbers obedient to certain laws; but why they obey these laws he cannot understand; and the fact of his not being able so to do, tends to give to numbers an atmosphere of mystery which impresses him with awe.

For instance, the property of the number 9, discovered, I believe, by W. Green, who died in 1794, is inexplicable to any one but a mathematician. The property to which I allude is this, that when 9 is multiplied by 2, by 3, by 4, by 5, by 6, &c., it will be found that the digits composing the product, when added together, give 9. Thus:—

$$2 \times 9 = 18, \quad \text{and} \quad 1 + 8 = 9$$
$$3 \times 9 = 27, \quad \text{“} \quad 2 + 7 = 9$$
$$4 \times 9 = 36, \quad \text{“} \quad 3 + 6 = 9$$
$$5 \times 9 = 45, \quad \text{“} \quad 4 + 5 = 9$$
$$6 \times 9 = 54, \quad \text{“} \quad 5 + 4 = 9$$
$$7 \times 9 = 63, \quad \text{“} \quad 6 + 3 = 9$$
$$8 \times 9 = 72, \quad \text{“} \quad 7 + 2 = 9$$
$$9 \times 9 = 81, \quad \text{“} \quad 8 + 1 = 9$$
$$10 \times 9 = 90, \quad \text{“} \quad 9 + 0 = 9$$

It will be noticed that 9×11 makes 99, the sum of the digits of which is 18 and not 9, but the sum of the digits 1×8 equals 9.

$$9 \times 12 = 108, \text{ and } 1 + 0 + 8 = 9$$
$$9 \times 13 = 117, \text{ " } 1 + 1 + 7 = 9$$
$$9 \times 14 = 126, \text{ " } 1 + 2 + 6 = 9$$

And so on to any extent.

M. de Maivan discovered another singular property of the same number. If the order of the digits expressing a number be changed, and this number be subtracted from the former, the remainder will be 9 or a multiple of 9, and, being a multiple, the sum of its digits will be 9.

For instance, take the number 21, reverse the digits, and you have 12; subtract 12 from 21, and the remainder is 9. Take 63, reverse the digits, and subtract 36 from 63; you have 27, a multiple of 9, and 2 + 7 = 9. Once more, the number 13 is the reverse of 31; the difference between these numbers is 18, or twice 9.

Again, the same property found in two numbers thus changed, is discovered in the same numbers raised to any power.

Take 21 and 12 again. The square of 21 is 441, and the square of 12 is 144; subtract 144 from 441, and the remainder is 297, a multiple of 9; besides, the digits expressing these powers added together give 9. The cube of 21 is 9261, and that of 12 is 1728; their difference is 7533, also a multiple of 9.

The number 37 has also somewhat remarkable properties; when multiplied by 3 or a multiple of 3 up to 27, it gives in the product three digits exactly similar. From the knowledge of this the multiplication of 37 is greatly facilitated, the method to be adopted being to multiply merely the first cipher of the multiplicand by the first multiplier; it is then unnecessary to proceed with the multiplication, it being sufficient to write twice to the right hand the cipher obtained, so that the same digit will stand in the unit, tens, and hundreds places.

For instance, take the results of the following table:—

37 multiplied by   3 gives   111,   and   3 times   1 = 3

37   "   6   "   222,   "   3   "   2 = 6

37	"	9	"	333,	"	3	"	3 = 9
37	"	12	"	444,	"	3	"	4 = 12
37	"	15	"	555,	"	3	"	5 = 15
37	"	18	"	666,	"	3	"	6 = 18
37	"	21	"	777,	"	3	"	7 = 21
37	"	24	"	888,	"	3	"	8 = 24
37	"	27	"	999,	"	3	"	9 = 27

The singular property of numbers the most different, when added, to produce the same sum, originated the use of magical squares for talismans. Although the reason may be accounted for mathematically, yet numerous authors have written concerning them, as though there were something "uncanny" about them. But the most remarkable and exhaustive treatise on the subject is that by a mathematician of Dijon, which is entitled "Traité complet des Carrés magiques, pairs et impairs, simple et composés, à Bordures, Compartiments, Croix, Chassis, Équerres, Bandes détachées, &c.; suivi d'un Traité des Cubes magiques et d'un Essai sur les Cercles magiques; par M. Violle, Géomètre, Chevalier de St. Louis, avec Atlas de 54 grandes Feuilles, comprenant 400 figures." Paris, 1837. 2 vols. 8vo., the first of 593 pages, the second of 616. Price 36 fr.

I give three examples of magical squares:—

$$2\ 7\ 6$$
$$9\ 5\ 1$$
$$4\ 3\ 8$$

These nine ciphers are disposed in three horizontal lines; add the three ciphers of each line, and the sum is 15; add the three ciphers in each column, the sum is 15; add the three ciphers forming diagonals, and the sum is 15.

$$1\ \ 2\ 3\ 4$$
$$2\ \ 3\ 2\ 3$$
$$4\ \ 1\ 4\ 1$$
$$122$$

$$3 \quad 4 \quad 1 \quad 2$$

The sum is 10.

1	7	13	19	25
18	24	5	6	12
10	11	17	23	4
22	3	9	15	16
14	20	21	2	8

The sum is 65.

But the connection of certain numbers with the dogmas of religion was sufficient, besides their marvellous properties, to make superstition attach itself to them. Because there were thirteen at the table when the Last Supper was celebrated, and one of the number betrayed his Master, and then hung himself, it is looked upon through Christendom as unlucky to sit down thirteen at table, the consequence being that one of the number will die before the year is out. "When I see," said Vouvenargues, "men of genius not daring to sit down thirteen at table, there is no error, ancient or modern, which astonishes me."

Nine, having been consecrated by Buddhism, is regarded with great veneration by the Moguls and Chinese: the latter bow nine times on entering the presence of their Emperor.

Three is sacred among Brahminical and Christian people, because of the Trinity of the Godhead.

Pythagoras taught that each number had its own peculiar character, virtue, and properties.

"The unit, or the monad," he says, "is the principle and the end of all; it is this sublime knot which binds together the chain of causes; it is the symbol of identity, of equality, of existence, of conservation, and of general harmony. Having no parts, the monad represents Divinity; it announces also order, peace, and tranquillity, which are founded on unity of sentiments; consequently One is a good principle.

"The number Two, or the dyad, the origin of contrasts, is the symbol of diversity, or inequality, of division and of separation. Two is accordingly an evil principle, a number of bad augury, characterizing disorder, confusion, and change.

"Three, or the triad, is the first of unequals; it is the number containing the most sublime mysteries, for everything is composed of three substances; it represents God, the soul of the world, the spirit of man." This number, which plays so great a part in the traditions of Asia, and in the Platonic philosophy, is the image of the attributes of God.

"Four, or the tetrad, as the first mathematical power, is also one of the chief elements; it represents the generating virtue, whence come all combinations; it is the most perfect of numbers; it is the root of all things. It is holy by nature, since it constitutes the Divine essence, by recalling His unity, His power, His goodness, and His wisdom, the four perfections which especially characterize God. Consequently, Pythagoricians swear by the quaternary number, which gives the human soul its eternal nature.

"The number Five, or the pentad, has a peculiar force in sacred expiations; it is everything; it stops the power of poisons, and is redoubted by evil spirits.

"The number Six, or the hexad, is a fortunate number, and it derives its merit from the first sculptors having divided the face into six portions; but, according to the Chaldeans, the reason is, because God created the world in six days.

"Seven, or the heptad, is a number very powerful for good or for evil. It belongs especially to sacred things.

"The number Eight, or the octad, is the first cube, that is to say, squared in all senses, as a die, proceeding from its base two, an even number; so is man four-square, or perfect.

"The number Nine, or the ennead, being the multiple of three, should be regarded as sacred.

"Finally, Ten, or the decad, is the measure of all, since it contains all the numeric relations and harmonies. As the reunion of the four first numbers, it plays an eminent part, since all the branches of science, all nomenclatures, emanate from, and retire into it."

It is hardly necessary for me here to do more than mention the peculiar character given to different numbers by Christianity. One is the numeral indicating the Unity of the Godhead; Two points to the hypostatic union; Three to the Blessed Trinity; Four to the Evangelists; Five to the Sacred Wounds; Six is the number of sin; Seven that of the gifts of the Spirit; Eight, that of the Beatitudes; Ten is the number of the commandments; Eleven speaks of the Apostles after the loss of Judas; Twelve, of the complete apostolic college.

I shall now point out certain numbers which have been regarded with superstition, and certain events connected with numbers which are of curious interest.

The number 14 has often been observed as having singularly influenced the life of Henry IV. and other French princes. Let us take the history of Henry.

On the 14th May, 1029, the first king of France named Henry was consecrated, and on the 14th May, 1610, the last Henry was assassinated.

Fourteen letters enter into the composition of the name of Henri de Bourbon, who was the 14th king bearing the titles of France and Navarre.

The 14th December, 1553, that is, 14 centuries, 14 decades, and 14 years after the birth of Christ, Henry IV. was born; the ciphers of the date 1553, when added together, giving the number 14.

The 14th May, 1554, Henry II. ordered the enlargement of the Rue de la Ferronnerie. The circumstance of this order not having been carried out, occasioned the murder of Henry IV. in that street, four times 14 years after.

The 14th May, 1552, was the date of the birth of Marguérite de Valois, first wife of Henry IV.

On the 14th May, 1588, the Parisians revolted against Henry III., at the instigation of the Duke of Guise.

On the 14th March, 1590, Henry IV. gained the battle of Ivry.

On the 14th May, 1590, Henry was repulsed from the Fauxbourgs of Paris.

On the 14th November, 1590, the Sixteen took oath to die rather than serve Henry.

On the 14th November, 1592, the Parliament registered the Papal Bull giving power to the legate to nominate a king to the exclusion of Henry.

On the 14th December, 1599, the Duke of Savoy was reconciled to Henry IV.

On the 14th September, 1606, the Dauphin, afterwards Louis XIII., was baptized.

On the 14th May, 1610, the king was stopped in the Rue de la Ferronnerie, by his carriage becoming locked with a cart, on account of the narrowness of the street. Ravaillac took advantage of the occasion for stabbing him.

Henry IV. lived four times 14 years, 14 weeks, and four times 14 days; that is to say, 56 years and 5 months.

On the 14th May, 1643, died Louis XIII., son of Henry IV.; not only on the same day of the same month as his father, but the date, 1643, when its ciphers are added together, gives the number 14, just as the ciphers of the date of the birth of his father gave 14.

Louis XIV. mounted the throne in 1643: $1 + 6 + 4 + 3 = 14$.

He died in the year 1715: $1 + 7 + 1 + 5 = 14$.

He lived 77 years, and $7 + 7 = 14$.

Louis XV. mounted the throne in the same year; he died in 1774, which also bears the stamp of 14, the extremes being 14, and the sum of the means $7 + 7$ making 14.

Louis XVI. had reigned 14 years when he convoked the States General, which was to bring about the Revolution.

The number of years between the assassination of Henry IV. and the dethronement of Louis XVI. is divisible by 14.

Louis XVII. died in 1794; the extreme digits of the date are 14, and the first two give his number.

The restoration of the Bourbons took place in 1814, also marked by the extremes being 14; also by the sum of the ciphers making 14.

The following are other curious calculations made respecting certain French kings.

Add the ciphers composing the year of the birth or of the death of some of the kings of the third race, and the result of each sum is the titular number of each prince. Thus:—

Louis IX. was born in 1215; add the four ciphers of this date, and you have IX.

Charles VII. was born in 1402; the sum of $1 + 4 + 2$ gives VII.

Louis XII. was born in 1461; and $1 + 4 + 6 + 1 = $ XII.

Henry IV. died in 1610; and $1 + 6 + 1 = $ twice IV.

Louis XIV. was crowned in 1643; and these four ciphers give XIV. The same king died in 1715; and this date gives also XIV. He was aged 77 years, and again $7 + 7 = 14$.

Louis XVIII. was born in 1755; add the digits, and you have XVIII.

What is remarkable is, that this number 18 is double the number of the king to whom the law first applies, and is triple the number of the kings to whom it has applied.

Here is another curious calculation:—

Robespierre fell in 1794;

Napoleon in 1815, and Charles X. in 1830.

Now, the remarkable fact in connection with these dates is, that the sum of the digits composing them, added to the dates, gives the date of the fall of the successor. Robespierre fell in 1794; $1 + 7 + 9 + 4 = 21$, $1794 + 21 = 1815$, the date of the fall of Napoleon; $1 + 8 + 1 + 5 = 15$, and $1815 + 15 = 1830$, the date of the fall of Charles X.

There is a singular rule which has been supposed to determine the length of the reigning Pope's life, in the earlier half of a century. Add his number to that of his predecessor, to that add ten, and the result gives the year of his death.

Pius VII. succeeded Pius VI.; $6 + 7 = 13$; add 10, and the sum is 23. Pius VII. died in 1823.

Leo XII. succeeded Pius VII.; $12 + 7 + 10 = 29$; and Leo XII. died in 1829.

Pius VIII. succeeded Leo XII.; $8 + 12 + 10 = 30$; and Pius VIII. died in 1830.

However, this calculation does not always apply.

Gregory XVI. ought to have died in 1834, but he did not actually vacate his see till 1846.

It is also well known that an ancient tradition forbids the hope of any of St. Peter's successors, *pervenire ad annos Petri*; i. e., to reign 25 years.

Those who sat longest are

		Years.	Months.	Days.
Pius VI.,	who reigned	24	6	14
Hadrian I.	"	23	10	17
Pius VII.	"	23	5	6
Alexander III.	"	21	11	23
St. Silvester I.	"	21	0	4

There is one numerical curiosity of a very remarkable character, which I must not omit.

The ancient Chamber of Deputies, such as it existed in 1830, was composed of 402 members, and was divided into two parties. The one, numbering 221 members, declared itself strongly for the revolution of July; the other party, numbering 181, did not favor a change. The result was the constitutional monarchy, which re-established order after the three memorable days of July. The parties were known by the following nicknames. The larger was commonly called La queue de Robespierre, and the smaller, Les honnêtes gens. Now, the remarkable fact is, that if we give to the letters of the alphabet their numerical values as they stand in their order, as 1 for A, 2 for B, 3 for C, and so on to Z, which is valued at 25, and then write vertically on the left hand the words, La queue de Robespierre, with the number equivalent to each letter opposite to it, and on the right hand, in like manner, Les honnêtes gens, if each column of numbers be summed up, the result is the number of members who formed each party.

1 2 3 4 5 6 7 8 9 10 11 12 13

A B C D E F G H I J K L M

14 15 16 17 18 19 20 21 22 23 24 25

N O P Q R S T U V X Y Z

L—12   L—12
A— 1   E— 5
        S—19

Q—17
U—21   H— 8
E— 5   O—15
U— 5   N—14
E— 5   N—14
        E— 5
D— 4   T—20
E— 5   E— 5
        S—19
R—18
O—15   G— 7
B— 2   E— 5
E— 5   N—14
S—19   S—19
P—16   181
I— 9
E— 5
R—18
R—18
E— 5
221

Majority 221

Minority 181

Total   402

Some coincidences of dates are very remarkable.

On the 25th August, 1569, the Calvinists massacred the Catholic nobles and priests at Béarn and Navarre.

On the same day of the same month, in 1572, the Calvinists were massacred in Paris and elsewhere.

On the 25th October, 1615, Louis XIII. married Anne of Austria, infanta of Spain, whereupon we may remark the following coincidences:—

The name Loys[36] de Bourbon contains 13 letters; so does the name Anne d'Austriche.

Louis was 13 years old when this marriage was decided on; Anne was the same age.

He was the thirteenth king of France bearing the name of Louis, and she was the thirteenth infanta of the name of Anne of Austria.

On the 23d April, 1616, died Shakspeare: on the same day of the same month, in the same year, died the great poet Cervantes.

On the 29th May, 1630, King Charles II. was born.

On the 29th May, 1660, he was restored.

On the 29th May, 1672, the fleet was beaten by the Dutch.

On the 29th May, 1679, the rebellion of the Covenanters broke out in Scotland.

The Emperor Charles V. was born on February 24, 1500; on that day he won the battle of Pavia, in 1525, and on the same day was crowned in 1530.

On the 29th January, 1697, M. de Broquemar, president of the Parliament of Paris, died suddenly in that city; next day his brother, an officer, died suddenly at Bergue, where he was governor. The lives of these brothers present remarkable coincidences. One day the officer, being engaged in battle, was wounded in his leg by a

---

[36] Up to Louis XIII. all the kings of this name spelled Louis as Loys.

sword-blow. On the same day, at the same moment, the president was afflicted with acute pain, which attacked him suddenly in the same leg as that of his brother which had been injured.

John Aubrey mentions the case of a friend of his who was born on the 15th November; his eldest son was born on the 15th November; and his second son's first son on the same day of the same month.

At the hour of prime, April 6, 1327, Petrarch first saw his mistress Laura, in the Church of St. Clara in Avignon. In the same city, same month, same hour, 1348, she died.

The deputation charged with offering the crown of Greece to Prince Otho, arrived in Munich on the 13th October, 1832; and it was on the 13th October, 1862, that King Otho left Athens, to return to it no more.

On the 21st April, 1770, Louis XVI. was married at Vienna, by the sending of the ring.

On the 21st June, in the same year, took place the fatal festivities of his marriage.

On the 21st January, 1781, was the fête at the Hôtel de Ville, for the birth of the Dauphin.

On the 21st June, 1791, took place the flight to Varennes.

On the 21st January, 1793, he died on the scaffold.

There is said to be a tradition of Norman-monkish origin, that the number 3 is stamped on the Royal line of England, so that there shall not be more than three princes in succession without a revolution.

William I., William II., Henry I.; then followed the revolution of Stephen.

Henry II., Richard I., John; invasion of Louis, Dauphin of France, who claimed the throne.

Henry III., Edward I., Edward II., who was dethroned and put to death.

Edward III., Richard II., who was dethroned.

Henry IV., Henry V., Henry VI.; the crown passed to the house of York.

Edward IV., Edward V., Richard III.; the crown claimed and won by Henry Tudor.

Henry VII., Henry VIII., Edward VI.; usurpation of Lady Jane Grey.

Mary I., Elizabeth; the crown passed to the house of Stuart.

James I., Charles I.; Revolution.

Charles II., James II.; invasion of William of Orange.

William of Orange and Mary II., Anne; arrival of the house of Brunswick.

George I., George II., George III., George IV., William IV., Victoria. The law has proved faulty in the last case; but certainly there was a crisis in the reign of George IV.

As I am on the subject of the English princes, I will add another singular coincidence, though it has nothing to do with the fatality of numbers.

It is that Saturday has been a day of ill omen to the later kings.

William of Orange died Saturday, 18th March, 1702.

Anne died Saturday, 1st August, 1704.

George I. died Saturday, 10th June, 1727.

George II. died Saturday, 25th October, 1760.

George III. died Saturday, 30th January, 1820.

George IV. died Saturday, 26th June, 1830.

THE TERRESTRIAL PARADISE

THE exact position of Eden, and its present condition, do not seem to have occupied the minds of our Anglo-Saxon ancestors, nor to have given rise among them to wild speculations.

The map of the tenth century in the British Museum, accompanying the Periegesis of Priscian, is far more correct than the generality of maps which we find in MSS. at a later period; and Paradise does not occupy the place of Cochin China, or the isles of Japan, as it did later, after that the fabulous voyage of St. Brandan had become popular in the eleventh century.[37] The site, however, had been already indicated by Cosmas, who wrote in the seventh century, and had been specified by him as occupying a continent east of China, beyond the ocean, and still watered by the four great rivers Pison, Gihon, Hiddekel, and Euphrates, which sprang from subterranean canals. In a map of the ninth century, preserved in the Strasbourg library, the terrestrial Paradise is, however, on the Continent, placed at the extreme east of Asia; in fact, is situated in the Celestial Empire. It occupies the same position in a Turin MS., and also in a map accompanying a commentary on the Apocalypse in the British Museum.

According to the fictitious letter of Prester John to the Emperor Emanuel Comnenus, Paradise was situated close to—within three days' journey of—his own territories, but where those territories were, is not distinctly specified.

"The River Indus, which issues out of Paradise," writes the mythical king, "flows among the plains, through a certain province, and it expands, embracing the whole province with its various

---

[37] St. Brandan was an Irish monk, living at the close of the sixth century; he founded the Monastery of Clonfert, and is commemorated on May 16. His voyage seems to be founded on that of Sinbad, and is full of absurdities. It has been republished by M. Jubinal from MSS. in the Bibliothèque du Roi, Paris, 8vo. 1836; the earliest printed English edition is that of Wynkyn de Worde, London, 1516.

windings: there are found emeralds, sapphires, carbuncles, topazes, chrysolites, onyx, beryl, sardius, and many other precious stones. There too grows the plant called Asbetos." A wonderful fountain, moreover, breaks out at the roots of Olympus, a mountain in Prester John's domain, and "from hour to hour, and day by day, the taste of this fountain varies; and its source is hardly three days' journey from Paradise, from which Adam was expelled. If any man drinks thrice of this spring, he will from that day feel no infirmity, and he will, as long as he lives, appear of the age of thirty." This Olympus is a corruption of Alumbo, which is no other than Columbo in Ceylon, as is abundantly evident from Sir John Mandeville's Travels; though this important fountain has escaped the observation of Sir Emmerson Tennant.

"Toward the heed of that forest (he writes) is the cytee of Polombe, and above the cytee is a great mountayne, also clept Polombe. And of that mount, the Cytee hathe his name. And at the foot of that Mount is a fayr welle and a gret, that hathe odour and savour of all spices; and at every hour of the day, he chaungethe his odour and his savour dyversely. And whoso drynkethe 3 times fasting of that watre of that welle, he is hool of alle maner sykenesse, that he hathe. And thei that duellen there and drynken often of that welle, thei nevere han sykenesse, and thei semen alle weys yonge. I have dronken there of 3 of 4 sithes; and zit, methinkethe, I fare the better. Some men clepen it the Welle of Youthe: for thei that often drynken thereat, semen alle weys yongly, and lyven withouten sykenesse. And men seyn, that that welle comethe out of Paradys: and therefore it is so vertuous."

Gautier de Metz, in his poem on the "Image du Monde," written in the thirteenth century, places the terrestrial Paradise in an unapproachable region of Asia, surrounded by flames, and having an armed angel to guard the only gate.

Lambertus Floridus, in a MS. of the twelfth century, preserved in the Imperial Library in Paris, describes it as "Paradisus insula in oceano in oriente:" and in the map accompanying it, Paradise is represented as an island, a little south-east of Asia, surrounded by rays, and at some distance from the main land; and in another MS. of the same library,—a mediæval encyclopædia,—under the word

Paradisus is a passage which states that in the centre of Paradise is a fountain which waters the garden—that in fact described by Prester John, and that of which story-telling Sir John Mandeville declared he had "dronken 3 or 4 sithes." Close to this fountain is the Tree of Life. The temperature of the country is equable; neither frosts nor burning heats destroy the vegetation. The four rivers already mentioned rise in it. Paradise is, however, inaccessible to the traveller on account of the wall of fire which surrounds it.

Paludanus relates in his "Thesaurus Novus," of course on incontrovertible authority, that Alexander the Great was full of desire to see the terrestrial Paradise, and that he undertook his wars in the East for the express purpose of reaching it, and obtaining admission into it. He states that on his nearing Eden an old man was captured in a ravine by some of Alexander's soldiers, and they were about to conduct him to their monarch, when the venerable man said, "Go and announce to Alexander that it is in vain he seeks Paradise; his efforts will be perfectly fruitless; for the way of Paradise is the way of humility, a way of which he knows nothing. Take this stone and give it to Alexander, and say to him, 'From this stone learn what you must think of yourself.'" Now, this stone was of great value and excessively heavy, outweighing and excelling in value all other gems; but when reduced to powder, it was as light as a tuft of hay, and as worthless. By which token the mysterious old man meant, that Alexander alive was the greatest of monarchs, but Alexander dead would be a thing of nought.

That strangest of mediæval preachers, Meffreth, who got into trouble by denying the Immaculate Conception of the Blessed Virgin, in his second sermon for the Third Sunday in Advent, discusses the locality of the terrestrial Paradise, and claims St. Basil and St. Ambrose as his authorities for stating that it is situated on the top of a very lofty mountain in Eastern Asia; so lofty indeed is the mountain, that the waters of the four rivers fall in cascade down to a lake at its foot, with such a roar that the natives who live on the shores of the lake are stone-deaf. Meffreth also explains the escape of Paradise from submergence at the Deluge, on the same grounds as does the Master of Sentences (lib. 2, dist. 17, c. 5), by the mountain being so very high that the waters which rose over Ararat were only able to wash the base of the mountain of Paradise.

The Hereford map of the thirteenth century represents the terrestrial Paradise as a circular island near India, cut off from the continent not only by the sea, but also by a battlemented wall, with a gateway to the west.

Rupert of Duytz regards it as having been situated in Armenia. Radulphus Highden, in the thirteenth century, relying on the authority of St. Basil and St. Isidore of Seville, places Eden in an inaccessible region of Oriental Asia; and this was also the opinion of Philostorgus. Hugo de St. Victor, in his book "De Situ Terrarum," expresses himself thus: "Paradise is a spot in the Orient productive of all kind of woods and pomiferous trees. It contains the Tree of Life: there is neither cold nor heat there, but perpetual equable temperature. It contains a fountain which flows forth in four rivers."

Rabanus Maurus, with more discretion, says, "Many folk want to make out that the site of Paradise is in the east of the earth, though cut off by the longest intervening space of ocean or earth from all regions which man now inhabits. Consequently, the waters of the Deluge, which covered the highest points of the surface of our orb, were unable to reach it. However, whether it be there, or whether it be anywhere else, God knows; but that there was such a spot once, and that it was on earth, that is certain."

Jacques de Vitry ("Historia Orientalis"), Gervais of Tilbury, in his "Otia Imperalia," and many others, hold the same views, as to the site of Paradise, that were entertained by Hugo de St. Victor.

Jourdain de Sèverac, monk and traveller in the beginning of the fourteenth century, places the terrestrial Paradise in the "Third India;" that is to say, in trans-Gangic India.

Leonardo Dati, a Florentine poet of the fifteenth century, composed a geographical treatise in verse, entitled "Della Sfera;" and it is in Asia that he locates the garden: —

> "Asia e le prima parte dove l'huomo
> Sendo innocente stava in Paradiso."

But perhaps the most remarkable account of the terrestrial Paradise ever furnished, is that of the "Eireks Saga Vídförla," an Icelandic narrative of the fourteenth century, giving the adventures of a certain Norwegian, named Eirek, who had vowed, whilst a heathen, that he would explore the fabulous Deathless Land of pagan Scandinavian mythology. The romance is possibly a Christian recension of an ancient heathen myth; and Paradise has taken the place in it of Glœsisvellir.

According to the majority of the MSS. the story purports to be nothing more than a religious novel; but one audacious copyist has ventured to assert that it is all fact, and that the details are taken down from the lips of those who heard them from Eirek himself. The account is briefly this:—

Eirek was a son of Thrand, king of Drontheim, and having taken upon him a vow to explore the Deathless Land, he went to Denmark, where he picked up a friend of the same name as himself. They then went to Constantinople, and called upon the Emperor, who held a long conversation with them, which is duly reported, relative to the truths of Christianity and the site of the Deathless Land, which, he assures them, is nothing more nor less than Paradise.

"The world," said the monarch, who had not forgotten his geography since he left school, "is precisely 180,000 stages round (about 1,000,000 English miles), and it is not propped up on posts— not a bit!—it is supported by the power of God; and the distance between earth and heaven is 100,045 miles (another MS. reads 9382 miles—the difference is immaterial); and round about the earth is a big sea called Ocean." "And what's to the south of the earth?" asked Eirek. "O! there is the end of the world, and that is India." "And pray where am I to find the Deathless Land?" "That lies— Paradise, I suppose, you mean—well, it lies slightly east of India."

Having obtained this information, the two Eireks started, furnished with letters from the Greek Emperor.

They traversed Syria, and took ship—probably at Balsora; then, reaching India, they proceeded on their journey on horseback, till they came to a dense forest, the gloom of which was so great, through the interlacing of the boughs, that even by day the stars could be observed twinkling, as though they were seen from the bottom of a well.

On emerging from the forest, the two Eireks came upon a strait, separating them from a beautiful land, which was unmistakably Paradise; and the Danish Eirek, intent on displaying his scriptural knowledge, pronounced the strait to be the River Pison. This was crossed by a stone bridge, guarded by a dragon.

The Danish Eirek, deterred by the prospect of an encounter with this monster, refused to advance, and even endeavored to persuade his friend to give up the attempt to enter Paradise as hopeless, after that they had come within sight of the favored land. But the Norseman deliberately walked, sword in hand, into the maw of the dragon, and next moment, to his infinite surprise and delight, found himself liberated from the gloom of the monster's interior, and safely placed in Paradise.

"The land was most beautiful, and the grass as gorgeous as purple; it was studded with flowers, and was traversed by honey rills. The land was extensive and level, so that there was not to be seen mountain or hill, and the sun shone cloudless, without night and darkness; the calm of the air was great, and there was but a feeble murmur of wind, and that which there was, breathed redolent with the odor of blossoms." After a short walk, Eirek observed what certainly must have been a remarkable object, namely, a tower or steeple self-suspended in the air, without any support whatever, though access might be had to it by means of a slender ladder. By this Eirek ascended into a loft of the tower, and found there an excellent cold collation prepared for him. After having partaken of this he went to sleep, and in vision beheld and conversed with his guardian angel, who promised to conduct him back to his fatherland, but to come for him again and fetch him away from it forever at the expiration of the tenth year after his return to Dronheim.

Eirek then retraced his steps to India, unmolested by the dragon, which did not affect any surprise at having to disgorge him, and, indeed, which seems to have been, notwithstanding his looks, but a harmless and passive dragon.

After a tedious journey of seven years, Eirek reached his native land, where he related his adventures, to the confusion of the heathen, and to the delight and edification of the faithful. "And in the tenth year, and at break of day, as Eirek went to prayer, God's Spirit caught him away, and he was never seen again in this world: so here ends all we have to say of him."[38]

The saga, of which I have given the merest outline, is certainly striking, and contains some beautiful passages. It follows the commonly-received opinion which identified Paradise with Ceylon; and, indeed, an earlier Icelandic work, the "Rymbegla," indicates the locality of the terrestrial Paradise as being near India, for it speaks of the Ganges as taking its rise in the mountains of Eden. It is not unlikely that the curious history of Eirek, if not a Christianized version of a heathen myth, may contain the tradition of a real expedition to India, by one of the hardy adventurers who overran Europe, explored the north of Russia, harrowed the shores of Africa, and discovered America.

Later than the fifteenth century, we find no theories propounded concerning the terrestrial Paradise, though there are many treatises on the presumed situation of the ancient Eden. At Madrid was published a poem on the subject, entitled "Patriana decas," in 1629. In 1662 G. C. Kirchmayer, a Wittemberg professor, composed a thoughtful dissertation, "De Paradiso," which he inserted in his "Deliciæ Æstivæ." Fr. Arnoulx wrote a work on Paradise in 1665, full of the grossest absurdities. In 1666 appeared Carver's "Discourse on the Terrestrian Paradise." Bochart composed a tract on the subject; Huet wrote on it also, and his work passed through seven editions, the last dated from Amsterdam, 1701. The Père Hardouin composed a "Nouveau Traité de la Situation du Paradis Terrestre," La Haye, 1730. An Armenian work on the rivers of Paradise was translated by M. Saint Marten in 1819; and in 1842 Sir W. Ouseley read a paper on the situation of Eden, before the Literary Society in London.

THE END

---

[38] Compare with this the death of Sir Galahad in the "Morte d'Arthur" of Sir Thomas Malory.